Goddess Girls

ATHENA
THE
PROUD

Goddess Girls

ATHENA
THE
PROUD

JOAN HOLUB & SUZANNE WILLIAMS

Aladdin

NEW YORK   LONDON   TORONTO   SYDNEY   NEW DELHI

ALADDIN

An imprint of Simon & Schuster Children's Publishing Division

1230 Avenue of the Americas, New York, NY 10020

First Aladdin hardcover edition April 2014

Text copyright © 2014 by Joan Holub and Suzanne Williams

Jacket illustration copyright © 2014 by Glen Hanson

Also available in an Aladdin paperback edition.

For information about special discounts for bulk purchases, please contact Simon & Schuster Special Sales at 1-866-506-1949 or business@simonandschuster.com.

The Simon & Schuster Speakers Bureau can bring authors to your live event. For more information or to book an event, contact the Simon & Schuster Speakers Bureau at 1-866-248-3049 or visit our website at www.simonspeakers.com.

Jacket designed by Karin Paprocki

Interior designed by Hilary Zarycky

The text of this book was set in Baskerville Handcut.

Manufactured in the United States of America 0314 FFG

2 4 6 8 10 9 7 5 3 1

Library of Congress Control Number 2014931058

ISBN 978-1-4424-8821-2 (hc)

ISBN 978-1-4424-8820-5 (pbk)

ISBN 978-1-4424-8822-9 (eBook)

2/4/14

A big thank-you to our a-MAZE-ing readers!
–J. H. and S. W.

CONTENTS

Goddess Girls

ATHENA
THE
PROUD

1

An Invitation

*P*ING! PING! ATHENA SLID INTO HER SEAT IN HER Beast-ology class at Mount Olympus Academy just as the lyrebell for second period rang. She pushed her long wavy brown hair back as she pulled her textscroll for the class from her bag.

Right away her dragon-headed teacher, Professor Ladon, held up a rolled sheet of papyrus. "An interesssting lettersssscroll hasss arrived, which I will now read aloud sssince it concernsss sssome of you," he announced to the class. Licks of flame flew from his lips as he spoke, setting the edge of the letterscroll on fire.

"Godnesss!" he exclaimed. The teacher's eyes bugged, and he began shaking the letterscroll with one clawed green hand in an attempt to put out the flames.

Poseidon, a handsome godboy with pale turquoise skin and eyes, jumped from his seat in the front row. "Don't worry, Professor Ladon. I'm on it!" he called. He grasped the long handle of the trident he always carried and extended its drippy three-pronged end toward the letterscroll. As drops of water sprayed from the trident's prongs onto the papyrus, the flames quickly fizzled out.

"Thanksss," hissed Professor Ladon. He smiled, baring huge, sharp dragon teeth.

Athena's blue-gray eyes widened, and she drew back a little. The sight of those teeth never failed to startle her.

But Poseidon grinned back at the teacher, unfazed. "No problemo." As godboy of the sea, he was all about water. He loved tinkering with the fountains here at MOA, and had designed a magnificent water park with polished marble slides, gleaming fountains, and pools of turquoise water down on Earth.

"Asss I wasss about to sssay," the teacher continued, wisely holding the papyrus scroll farther away from his long flame-spewing dragon snout this time. "I will now read the letterssscroll.

"DEAR PROFESSSOR LADON,

I AM WRITING TO INVITE FOURTEEN

SSSTUDENTS TO BE GUESTSSS AT

THE GRAND OPENING OF MY NEW

AMUSSSEMENT PARK.

WHEN: THISSS SSSATURDAY.

WHO: PLEASSSE SSSELECT SSSEVEN

BOYSSS AND SSSEVEN GIRLSSS, A MIX

OF GODDESSSGIRLSSS, GODBOYSSS, AND

MORTALSSS. THISSS ISSS A SSSPECIAL

PREVIEW JUSSST FOR THEM. THEY WILL

HAVE THE PARK ALL TO THEMSSSELVES.

LOCATION: MY PALACE IN KNOSSSOSSS, ON

THE COASSST OF THE ISLAND OF CRETE,

JUSSST SSSOUTH OF GREECE. A MAP ISSS

ATTACHED.

YOURSSS TRULY,

KING MINOSSS

P.SSS. NO WEAPONSSS ALLOWED."

Murmurs of excitement rose from the class. Athena leaned over and whispered to Persephone, the pale-skinned, red-haired goddessgirl who sat next to her and was one of her three best friends. "Did you catch that article about Minos's new amusement park in yesterday's *Greekly Weekly News*?"

Persephone nodded. "Uh-huh," she said. "It sounds really a-*maze*-ing." Both girls giggled at her little joke.

The king had officially named his park Minos's aMAZEment Park because its central attraction was a cavelike labyrinth. Which was basically a simple maze with numerous passages that ran beneath the king's palace.

The park had been designed and built by Daedalus. He was the most famous mortal inventor and architect on Earth, yet he was only sixteen years old! As the goddessgirl of crafts, among other things, Athena was a keen inventor herself. In fact, one of her inventions—the olive—had proved so useful to some mortals in Greece that they'd named their city Athens after her. In a contest at MOA earlier that year, her olive had even beat out the water park Poseidon had invented.

"So which of us get to go?" asked a dark-haired, dark-eyed godboy named Apollo.

Good question, thought Athena. She caught Persephone's eye again and crossed her fingers. Persephone crossed hers back. Because who wouldn't want a chance to preview a fabulous new funpark?

Before Professor Ladon could answer the question, a godboy with a lizardlike tail turned to grin at Apollo. "Don't you already know who's going, Mr. Godboy of Prophecy?"

Everyone laughed, including Apollo. It was true he

was the godboy of prophecy, but apparently he hadn't foreseen the king's invitation. *Or* the names of the students who'd be going.

"To ansssswer Apollo'sss query," Professor Ladon replied at last, "I think it fair that I sssend only the top ssstudentsss from all of my classsesss to the park asss a reward for achievement."

The students closest to him inched their hands up to cover their noses and mouths as he spoke. Professor Ladon had the worst dragon breath of any teacher at MOA!

Without seeming to notice, the teacher went on. "Ssso anyone who hasss achieved the tenth Level of the Arrow may volunteer to go."

Persephone pumped her arm. "That means we're in! So are Aphrodite and Artemisss!" she whispered to Athena excitedly. Then she giggled. "Oops! Sorry. I guess the teacher's habit of hissing his *Ss* is catching."

"Yesss!" Athena agreed, giggling too.

However, Poseidon groaned. He and several other students who hadn't yet achieved the tenth level slumped in their seats at the teacher's news. Athena felt kind of sorry for them. But they'd be able to visit Minos's aMAZEment Park another time, since it would be open for years to come.

She and her three goddessgirl best friends had recently made it to the tenth level after an epic battle. They'd defeated a dozen monsters—tough opponents with sharp teeth and claws, and breath even more horrific than Professor Ladon's! Of course, the monsters hadn't been *real* beasts, only magical game projections created by the professor to challenge them in the Forest of the Beasts down on Earth.

The forest was where the goddessgirls had fought

the monsters to win the tenth level. The place where all students from Professor Ladon's classes practiced their hunting skills on the first Friday of every month. The rest of the time classes were held here at MOA in this very classroom.

Persephone turned to look back at Hades, godboy of the Underworld. He flashed her a smile. The two of them had been crushing on each other since forever. Looking at Professor Ladon, Hades asked, "When do we leave?" He and several of his godboy friends, including Apollo, had also reached the tenth level recently.

"After ssschool on Friday. We'll ssspend all day Sssaturday at the park, and return Sssaturday evening," Professor Ladon replied.

Then he explained how the invitation had come about. Apparently, Daedalus had been impressed with the Forest of the Beasts when Professor Ladon had showed it to him nearly a year ago. In fact, after studying the magical beasts the professor had created, Daedalus had been inspired to design a mechanical version of the Minotaur, one of the most terrifying of the forest beasts. It would inhabit King Minos's new labyrinth.

"To thank me for providing inssspiration for his mechanical Minotaur, Daedalusss convinced King Minosss to invite ssstudents from my classsses to the opening of the park," Professor Ladon said in conclusion.

A shiver ran down Athena's back as she thought about the Minotaur. There were actually three of them in the Forest, and each was huge and bull-like, standing upright however, with horns, clawed hands, hooves, and a gold ring in its snorting nose. Terrifying, indeed!

But she didn't have time to dwell on the matter of the Minotaur. Because the class moved on to studying the languages of the beasts, until the lyrebell rang.

Out in the hall after class ended, Athena, Persephone, Apollo, and Hades all high-fived one another. "This trip is going to be so fun," said Persephone.

"It'll be awesome!" Apollo enthused. "Just think—we'll be the first ones ever to try the rides."

The boys took off for their next classes still buzzing about the park, but the two girls waited outside the classroom until Aphrodite and Artemis showed up for third-period Beast-ology.

After Athena and Persephone shared the good news about the upcoming trip, the four girls grabbed each other in a group hug, jumping up and down in excitement.

"I can hardly believe I get to hang out with my GGBFFs

at a funpark this weekend instead of doing homework," said Athena.

Artemis, Persephone, and Aphrodite looked at her in confusion. "GGBFF?"

"Goddessgirl best friends forever," explained Athena. "I'm so excited that I just made it up by accident!"

Her friends giggled. "So who else will be going? Do we know?" Aphrodite asked, running a hand through her long, golden hair. It was threaded with pink ribbons that matched the sparkly pink chiton she was wearing. As befitted the goddessgirl of love and beauty, she was breathtakingly beautiful. Several boys passing by turned their heads to glance at her adoringly before continuing on to their classes. But to her credit Aphrodite hardly noticed. She might be beautiful, but she wasn't stuck-up about it.

"Apollo will be," Artemis informed them. She shifted

the bow and quiver of arrows slung over her shoulder, which she rarely went anywhere without. Her dark hair was done up in its usual cute twist and secured with a gold band, and she smoothed a curl back into the twist as she continued on. "He and Actaeon just earned their tenth Level of the Arrow last week."

"How lucky that they'll both be able to come," Athena replied. Apollo was Artemis's twin brother, and Actaeon was Artemis's crush. "Heracles will get to go too. And Pandora." Heracles was *Athena's* crush, and Pandora was her roommate in the girls' dorm on the fourth floor of MOA. So she knew that both had achieved the tenth level.

Maybe Heracles and I can sit together on the ride over, Athena thought with pleasure. Two weeks ago, they'd worked with other students to build a fabulous carousel inside the Immortal Marketplace—a mall halfway between MOA and Earth. Since then she'd gotten so busy with homework, Cheer, and other projects that she'd hardly spent any time with him.

"Ares is tenth level," said Aphrodite, mentioning her crush. "I think Medusa and Dionysus are too."

"Hmm. Let's see," said Artemis. She counted on her fingers. "That makes the four of us, on the girls' side, plus Medusa and Pandora. And Apollo, Ares, Actaeon, Hades, Heracles, and Dionysus on the boys' side. Six and six."

"So we're missing one girl and one boy to make up the group of fourteen that Minos invited in that letterscroll, right?" asked Persephone.

The lyrebell began to *ping*, signaling that third period was about to begin. "Yikes, better get going," said Aphrodite. While nudging Artemis into the classroom, she sent Athena and Persephone a little wave good-bye.

Athena waved back and nodded to Persephone. "Right. Good math," she said in answer to her friend's question. "According to the *Greekly Weekly News* the fun-park is huge. King Minos could have invited the whole school! But I suppose he must be thinking it's best to try out the rides with a small group first. Before the park opens to the public."

As the two girls separated and began to move in different directions toward their next classes, Persephone called back over her shoulder. "We're lucky we're part of the group that gets to go. I can't wait for this weekend!"

"Me either," Athena called back. It wasn't every day that they got an exclusive invitation to the park that mortals and immortals everywhere were talking about. Everyone had been counting the days till it opened.

She still hadn't heard who the seventh girl and seventh boy were by the end of the school day when she climbed the marble staircase to the girls' dorm. Pandora was sitting at her desk working but immediately turned to greet Athena when she entered the room they shared.

"Hi. Isn't the news about the park trip mega-awesome? What should we pack? Do you have much homework?"

"Not that much," said Athena, answering only one of her questions. That was usually enough to satisfy Pandora. Besides, the two girls would wind up talking all night if Athena tried to answer all of her mortal roommate's questions. She liked Pandora, but sometimes it was hard to get any real work done when she was around. That girl was so curious about everything and asked so many questions that her bangs were shaped like question marks!

Athena put her stuff away and settled at her desk, which was near the window, beyond her bed and wardrobe. On the opposite side of the room were Pandora's identical bed, wardrobe, and desk.

Inspired by the thought that she might get to meet Daedalus in a few days, Athena opened a drawer and pulled out a sheaf of papyrus. The she picked up her favorite ink-filled blue-feather quill pen and tapped it against her chin, thinking.

"Need some help?" Pandora asked eagerly. Quiet drove her crazy.

Athena looked over at her, unsure. "Yeah, I do, actually," she said after a few seconds. "In your opinion what's the least successful or least exciting thing I've ever invented?"

"The plow?" Pandora answered without hesitation.

Athena stared at her in surprise. "Really? But it's so useful." A tool she'd created to help farmers, its iron blade could break up the soil and cut furrows in the ground, into which seed could later be sown to grow crops.

Pandora cocked her head and wrinkled her nose a

little. "Don't you think it's kind of heavy and awkward, though? I overheard some farmers down on Earth complaining that it takes two people to operate it—one to push on the wooden handle from behind and another person harnessed in front to pull. Don't take this the wrong way, but compared to your olive, and inventions like the ship, chariot, flute, and trumpet, that plow is kind of dull. And boring, too."

"*Awkward, dull, and boring?* Gosh, tell me what you *really* think, roomie," Athena teased. She adored inventing new things, worked hard to perfect them, and was proud of each and every one of her inventions, big or small. So Pandora's criticisms stung. But then, Athena *had* asked for feedback.

She grinned, softening her words. "You make good points, though. Come to think of it, I have heard grumbling about that plow now and then." She had received plenty of praise for her other inventions—though, to be fair, she could understand why people would think using a plow was hot, sweaty, hard, and awkward work.

"Thanks for being honest," Athena said, letting go of her hurt feelings. "You've been a big help."

"You're welcome," said Pandora.

To Athena's relief her roomie soon announced that she was leaving for a while to hang out with Medusa, a snake-haired, green-skinned mortal MOA student. Now Athena could get some real work done! After her roommate left, Athena began to sketch new design ideas for improving what Pandora—and farmers, apparently, too—considered her most hard-to-use and boring invention. The plow.

But how could she improve it? Would a sharper blade help? More comfortable handles for pushing? Wheels? She sketched out each idea as it came to her, but just as quickly rejected those ideas, tossing her sketches over her shoulder until they littered the floor.

As she continued drawing, her frustration grew. Nothing she came up with seemed like it would improve her current design enough to make a difference in the ease of her invention's use. She was stumped. Fresh out of good ideas.

When a knock came at her door, she called out distractedly, "Yes?"

"Hello? It's me," Artemis said, opening the door and coming in. Her three dogs—a beagle named Amby, a greyhound named Nectar, and a bloodhound named Suez—pushed their way inside with her. "Yikes, sorry," said Artemis as the dogs trampled on the papers spread all over the floor.

"S'okay," Athena told her. "That's my throwaway pile." Somehow Nectar managed to poke his head through a sheet of papyrus that she had rolled up and twisted into a hoop to resemble a wheel. The girls laughed as he ran around shaking his head back and forth, trying to free himself.

"What's up?" Athena asked as Artemis took pity on Nectar and slipped the paper "wheel" off his neck. The dog rose on two hind legs, put its front paws on Artemis, and licked her cheek before going back to nosing around the room with his two companions.

Artemis gave him a pat and frowned at Athena. "What do you mean, what's up? Did you forget that a bunch of us are meeting at the Supernatural Market for shakes? To celebrate being picked to go to the aMAZEment Park in Crete? We talked about it at lunch, remember? You said you'd come. Aphrodite and Persephone are waiting for us outside in the courtyard."

"Ye gods!" Athena exclaimed, jumping up. "I did

forget!" A quick glance out the window showed that the sun was starting to go down. And the sundial in the courtyard informed her that she'd been working for three hours and had completely missed dinner. She waved to Persephone and Aphrodite, who were down below looking up at her window, then looked back at Artemis. "I've been so caught up in work that I totally lost track of time. I'm starving."

Artemis grinned, holding the door wide open. "Well, come on, then. No better place to get snacks and a shake than the Supernatural Market."

After scooping up the papers on the floor, Athena tossed them into her wastebasket. Then she, Artemis, and the three dogs left to meet up with Aphrodite and Persephone.

As the four goddessgirls hurried toward the market, Athena thought about Heracles. Since he was also going

on the Crete trip, he'd probably be at the market with the others. She could hardly wait to talk to him about the trip and tell him how excited she was about getting to meet such an illustrious inventor as Daedalus.

2

Theseus

WHEN ATHENA AND HER FRIENDS ARRIVED AT the Supernatural Market, Artemis stopped her three hounds outside its doors. "Sorry, guys. You know you aren't allowed inside the store. We'll be back soon, and I'll bring you some treats."

Amby, Athena's favorite, wiggled all over as she reached down and gave him a *Good-bye for now* pat. "See you later, Amby-gator," she told him. Then she

followed the other three goddessgirls into the market.

Once inside, the girls passed shelves of snacks and a rack filled with copies of the latest issue of *Teen Scrollazine.* "Hey," said Persephone, snatching a copy from the rack, "isn't that your Hero-ology hero on the cover?" She handed the scrollazine to Athena. The drawing showed a strong-looking, curly-haired mortal man. He was standing between a lovely, dark-haired woman and a handsome teenage boy. His muscled arms were around the shoulders of both, and there was a proud, happy look on his face.

Athena nodded. "Yes, that's Odysseus. With his wife Penelope and their son, Telemachus," she said excitedly.

"I wonder what he's up to," Persephone said. "Now that Mr. Cyclops has us studying our textscrolls in Hero-ology class lately, instead of using the game board, I mean."

Athena had successfully guided Odysseus through the Trojan War and back home again by moving a little three-inch-high figure of the hero around a game board in Hero-ology class. Just as other class members had done with *their* assigned heroes. The figures were like chess pieces. They weren't the actual heroes; they only represented them. But whatever happened to heroes on the game board also happened to them in real life down on Earth!

Athena glanced at the caption on the cover of the scrollazine: *Main Story: Odysseus at Home, page 4.* She flipped to the beginning of the article and quickly skimmed it. She was disappointed to see that it was mostly a fluff piece. There was hardly anything in the article about all the trials and tribulations—the many shipwrecks and encounters with man-eating giants and tricky sorceresses, for example—that she'd guided

Odysseus through. Such troubles had filled his ten-year journey (his *Odyssey*) home to Ithaca.

Instead the interviewer had asked him about day-to-day things for the article. Like, what was Odysseus's favorite meal? (Anything he didn't have to cook himself.) What was his favorite way to relax? (Juggling axes.) And what was one of his favorite memories? (His faithful dog, Argos, recognizing him and happily running over to greet Odysseus when he arrived home in disguise after the Trojan War.)

It was a pretty bland interview for a guy as heroic as Odysseus. Still, after ten years of war plus that ten-year trip home, maybe he was ready to give up the hero biz and just enjoy his home and family. He certainly deserved some downtime after all he'd been through!

"I'll go grab some nectar shakes for us," Aphrodite said before she split off from the other girls to head for the soda counter.

"Okay," Athena called after her. Spying Heracles at a big, round table at the back of the store, she set the scrollazine back on the rack. Then she hurried to catch up with Artemis and Persephone, who'd gone on ahead while she'd been reading.

Ares and Hades were also already at the table. Even though Heracles' back was to Athena, she could spot him easily. Because, as usual, he was wearing his lion-skin cape, whose jaws fit his head like a helmet. She'd really, really, *really* hoped to sit by him so it would be easy to talk. However, the chairs on either side of him were taken, one by Artemis's brother, Apollo. And the other by a boy sporting dreadlocks.

Athena had never seen the dreadlocks boy before, but she could tell he was mortal right away because his skin didn't shimmer. When immortals like her drank nectar, it made their skin take on a glittery tone. It didn't have the same effect on mortals, though.

Persephone must have seen Athena eyeing the chairs near Heracles, for suddenly she hopped up from where she was sitting with Hades, directly across the table from Heracles. "Take my chair," she offered. "I'll bring another one over so we can sit together." Persephone was thoughtful that way.

As soon as both girls were seated, Aphrodite arrived with a tray full of frothy nectar shakes with straws. When she set the tray down in the middle of the table, hands instantly reached for the shakes. Athena took a sip of the one she'd snagged, and gave Aphrodite a warm smile. "Yum. Thanks!"

At the sound of her voice, Heracles looked up. He'd been in rapt conversation with the dreadlocks boy and apparently hadn't even noticed her until that moment. But now his brown eyes sparkled at her. "Hi, Athena." He motioned toward the unknown boy. "Meet my cousin, Theseus. He just got here from his dad's—King Aegeus—in Athens a few minutes ago."

Athena smiled at Theseus. "Hi."

Why hadn't Heracles mentioned that his cousin was coming to visit? she wondered. Though she'd hardly seen her crush outside of classes during the past couple of weeks, they'd chatted in the hallways and during snippets of time in the classes they had together. There *had* been opportunities for him to tell her.

Theseus dipped his head at her, and his dreadlocks fell forward over his shoulders. "Yeah. Hi," he said.

Athena could see a family resemblance in the shape of the two boys' dark eyes, their identical square jaws, and their muscular builds. "So how long will you be here at MOA?" she asked Theseus before taking another sip of her shake. *Mmm.* Delicious! The pale shimmer of her skin brightened with every sip.

Theseus had taken a gulp of his shake at the same time. He winced as he swallowed, then explained, "Sorry. Brain freeze. We don't get shakes like these down on Earth. They're awesome!"

She waited for him to reply to her question, but he seemed to have forgotten all about it. Instead his head swung back to Heracles.

Persephone leaned over to her and murmured, "I heard him say he'd be here for two days. Leaving Friday."

"Thanks," said Athena. Hearing Theseus mention Zeus, who was her dad and also the principal of Mount Olympus Academy, her ears perked up.

"I've been to Zeus's new temple in Olympia," Theseus was saying to Heracles. "I saw the paintings of your heroic deeds there. You are way wicked, Cuz."

He was complimenting Heracles' twelve labors, in which he'd battled all kinds of creatures, from a many-headed Hydra to birds with razor-sharp beaks. Athena had actually helped him a lot with those labors, and the paintings in Zeus's temple had been copied from tapestries depicting those labors, which she'd woven as a gift to Heracles afterward. As she sipped her shake, she waited for Heracles to mention this, but instead he just waved off Theseus's praise. "It was nothing," he said humbly.

"Not true," Theseus insisted. "You're the greatest hero that ever lived!"

"Aw, no way," Heracles said. Though he seemed a little embarrassed at the praise, he was smiling. "Couldn't have done it without . . ."

Again Athena waited for him to say her name. But instead he lifted his enormous, heavy club to stand upright and twirled the handle end in his palm. "My trusty club," he finished.

For Zeus's sake! thought Athena, feeling more than a little hurt. She remembered the time they spent together completing those labors so fondly. It was when they'd become each other's crushes. But far be it from her to fish for a compliment.

"So," she said to Theseus, "what are you guys going to do while you're—"

But before she could finish her question, Theseus spoke right over the top of her. "I've got something I want to show you," he said to Heracles.

"Yeah? What?" Heracles asked.

"You'll see." His dark eyes twinkling, Theseus reached beneath his tunic and drew out a short silver sword with a golden handle. Though it was very shiny, it actually looked more like a toy sword than a real one. Was it even sharp?

"Do you like my sword?" he asked Heracles. "It was a present from my dad."

"Nice," said Heracles in an admiring tone.

Some of the other boys overheard and leaned over to look. "It's a little short for a sword, though, isn't it? Looks more like a dagger to me," commented Apollo.

Theseus frowned at him. "It's a *sword*."

"Oh. Okay," Apollo said amiably. He rolled his eyes where Theseus couldn't see, as if to say, *Get over yourself, mortal dude!* Then he turned away to teasingly scold Artemis, who was sitting on his other side and had just tried to sneak a sip of his shake.

"I know it's not as mighty a weapon as your club," Theseus admitted to Heracles. "But I bet it'll serve me well in battle if I ever get the chance to use it!"

Athena pursed her lips and shared a look with Persephone. What made boys so crazy about weapons and battles, anyway? These guys' favorite place to shop at the Immortal Marketplace was a store called Mighty Fighty. It sold all kinds of battle gear like shields, spears, and bows and arrows. When it came to that kind of stuff, these boys had one-track minds!

Theseus seemed to be in awe of his cousin Heracles and aspiring to become a hero just like him. She wondered if the boy carried his dagger with him everywhere, the way Artemis did her bow and arrows. And like Heracles used to do with his huge, knobby club until Athena had convinced him to leave it in his dorm room most of the time. The fact that he had it with him now made her wonder if he might be showing off a little for his cousin.

Persephone was busy chatting with Hades now as Aphrodite squeezed a chair between her and Athena. "Seems like we've hardly talked much lately," Aphrodite said to Athena as she sat down.

"I know, right?" Athena agreed, pushing her nearly empty shake away. "I've had homework, homework, homework. Not to mention our Cheer practice and some inventions I'm working on in my free time. How about you?"

"Swamped," said Aphrodite. "And not just with homework and Cheer. Remember that Lonely Hearts Club I started a while back, where mortals write to me asking for help with their love lives?"

Athena nodded. "Are you still doing that? Still getting letters, I mean?"

"Yeah, I never officially *stopped* doing it," Aphrodite said. "The letters died down for a while is all. But lately I've been getting more of them again. Just this morning I got one from a girl who wanted help getting her boyfriend back." Aphrodite arched a perfectly shaped eyebrow. "Sadly, I had to write her that it was probably too late for that."

"Why?" asked Athena.

"According to her letter she'd been so busy with her own activities that she'd been spending less and less time with him. Apparently they grew apart and he lost interest in her. Then he met another girl." Aphrodite shook her head as if to say she just didn't get why the girl had neglected her crush. "I always make time for Ares. I mean, why wouldn't I? Without time, relationships wither and die."

"Like plants without water," Persephone agreed. Hades was talking to the guys now, and she'd turned back to join the two girls' conversation.

"Makes sense," said Athena, thinking hard on what they'd said. As the goddessgirl of love and beauty, Aphrodite could be trusted to know what made relationships work. After all, she was an expert. And Athena trusted Persephone's opinion too. She and Hades got along great.

"Looks like we already need another round of shakes," Aphrodite said, gesturing toward the now empty tray.

"I'll get them this time," offered Athena. As she picked up the tray and went to the soda counter a few tables over to fetch more, Aphrodite's words echoed inside her head . . . *too late* . . . *lost interest*. She drew in a sharp breath. Could what had happened to that letter-writer-girl happen to *her*? she wondered. Was it already happening? Could her distraction and lack of attention be causing Heracles to lose interest in their friendship? That would be awful!

As she waited at the counter for the clerk to make more shakes, she remembered she was starving and bought two snack bars. Munching them, she happened to glance at a cheesy gossip scrollazine in the rack beside her. The cover headline read: *Love Tips from a Dumped*

Hydra-Gal! She unrolled the scrollazine and read more: *He said I had too many heads for business and too little time for him! Love dashed!* Alongside the words there was a picture of the seven-headed Hydra-lady, looking heartbroken.

Starting to feel anxious, Athena put the scrollazine back in the rack. Were her heads—um, *head*—so buried in homework and other stuff that she was pushing Heracles away? Was her love doomed to be dashed too? But maybe it wasn't too late to make amends. Determined to wrest Heracles' attention from Theseus, if only for a few minutes, she picked up the tray as soon as it was ready, and turned to hurry back toward the table.

Athena's heart sunk when she saw that the two boys were no longer sitting there. She glanced toward the front of the market just in time to see them go out the door. Heracles had left without even saying good-bye! That kind of hurt, and she was worried about what it might

mean.

Oh, stop it, she chided herself. *Everything's fine. Besides,*

Theseus is leaving in just two days. She and Heracles could

renew their friendship during the trip to Crete. It would

be great!

3

Stuck!

"HEY, PHEME!" ATHENA CALLED OUT TO THE goddessgirl of gossip, who'd just passed the table where Athena and Artemis were eating lunch the next day.

Pheme reversed direction and fluttered back to their table, her sandaled feet hovering a few inches above the floor. As her sandals touched down, her small, cute wings stilled. The glittery iridescent wings were a gift from Principal Zeus. A reward for heroism! Like her lip gloss and hair, they were orange, her favorite color.

"Artemis just told me you're tenth level in Professor Ladon's class. Eros, too," Athena told her. Those two were the missing seventh girl and seventh boy. "So are you excited about the funpark trip?" She used to go out of her way to avoid the gossipy girl, but that had changed not long ago. Pheme had been a big help when the two of them had worked together to rescue Phaeton, a brave but reckless boy with an obsession for chariots.

Before answering the question, Pheme glanced around the table and then asked one of her own. "Where are Aphrodite and Persephone? The four of you always eat lunch together. Was there an argu—"

"No argument," Athena said to head her off. The fact that Pheme was constantly on the lookout for good *and* ill rumors to spread had often bugged her in the past. Now she just dealt with it.

"They left a few minutes ago to check on Adonis," Artemis volunteered before taking a bite of her nectarburger. Adonis was a black-and-white kitten that Aphrodite and Persephone shared and took turns caring for.

"Oh," Pheme said, sounding a bit disappointed. Seeking out juicy gossip was sort of like her job at MOA. Plus, it gave her material for the gossip column she wrote in *Teen Scrollazine*, which was mega-popular with readers.

"You should've come to the Supernatural Market yesterday," said Artemis. "We were all buzzing about the park and what we're going to do there and stuff."

"Couldn't. I was packing," Pheme explai leave after school today for a journalism conf Athens." As always when she spoke, puffy clo formed above her head so that anyone who happ be looking up could read her words. "The whole staff of *Teen Scrollazine* is attending, along with *Greekly Weekly News* reporters and staff from lots of other magazines and newspapers."

"Sounds fun," said Athena. "You'll be back in time to go to the aMAZEment Park, though, won't you?"

The corners of Pheme's orange-glossed lips turned down. "Nope. I'll have to miss it. The conference goes through the weekend. I don't get home till Saturday evening, probably about the same time you guys get back." She stole an ambrosia fry from Athena's plate and munched it.

"Oh, too bad," said Athena, and Pheme nodded.

ıat's too bad?" asked Apollo, who'd just come over ıle. Without waiting for an answer, he nodded rtemis. "Hey, Sis. Don't forget we've got archery after school."

"I won't forget," Artemis assured him. Then she went back to what she'd been doing just before he arrived, namely, feeding her three dogs pieces of her nectarburger under the table.

"Pheme can't come to Crete," Athena told Apollo.

"Oh, rotten luck." He silently read the cloud letters that still lingered over Pheme's spiky orange-haired head, then looked at her. "So you're going to a conference instead?"

Pheme nodded. "It was a hard choice, but I couldn't pass up a chance to meet so many other reporters." She licked her lips. "Who knows what juicy tidbits I might learn?"

Apollo and Athena laughed. Pheme *lived* to gossip. It drove them all crazy sometimes and could also cause trouble. But it was as necessary to her as the ambrosia and nectar the immortal students at Mount Olympus

Academy ate and drank in order to stay immortal.

Suddenly Apollo's dark eyes lit up. "Hey," he said to Pheme, "since you can't go anyway, what would you think about asking Professor Ladon if Cassandra could go in your place?"

"Ooh! Great idea!" Athena exclaimed. Cassandra wasn't an MOA student, though. She went to school in the Immortal Marketplace, where her family owned and ran a bakery and scrollbook shop. Still, Athena felt like she owed the mortal girl a favor, so she was all for Apollo's suggestion. If it hadn't been for Cassandra's helpful predictions about Odysseus's future a couple of weeks ago, Athena might never have succeeded in guiding her hero back home to Ithaca. As return favors went, a trip to the most mega-mazing amusement park in Greece might just fill the bill.

Pheme cocked her head, considering. "I guess I

could ask. I like Cassandra. And her mom and I kind of bonded when we all helped with the grand opening of their family bookshop and I was doing the promotion."

"So we're agreed?" Apollo prodded Pheme. "You'll ask Professor Ladon?"

Maybe he felt he owed Cassandra a favor too, thought Athena. Years ago he'd accidentally put a curse on the girl. Because of that, no one ever believed her predictions—at least not for long. Apollo had tried to reverse the curse, but his attempt had been unsuccessful.

At least that problem had eventually been semi-resolved. Cassandra now had her very own line of Opposite Oracle-O cookies that were being sold in her family's store. The cookies' spoken or written predictions always foretold the *opposite* of what would actually happen, though. So when you opened one up, you only had to believe the opposite of whatever its fortune said, and that would turn out to be true.

"Sure," Pheme said. "I've got Beast-ology after lunch, so I'll ask him then."

"Awesome!" Apollo exclaimed. After saying good-bye to the girls, he walked off whistling a tune that Athena recognized as one of the mega-pop star Orpheus's newest releases. It was called, "I Predict You Love Me."

Athena and Pheme exchanged smiles. It was common knowledge that Apollo was crushing on Cassandra. Maybe *that* was why he wanted her to go with them to Crete, rather than to make up for the curse he'd put on her!

As the lyrebell sounded, Athena jumped up to take her leftovers to the tray return. Heracles had fourth-period Revenge-ology with her. If she hurried, maybe she'd get a chance to chat with him for a few minutes before class.

Unfortunately, it wound up that Ms. Nemesis was in a hurry to start her lesson that day. So Athena could only send Heracles a quick wave from across the room before taking her seat. Theseus was in the desk behind him. Looked like he would be attending classes with Heracles. Later, when the students split up into pairs briefly for an in-class assignment, Athena wound up working with Medusa, since Theseus nabbed Heracles as his partner first.

When the period ended, Pheme, who had Revengeology fifth period, came up to Athena just outside the classroom door. "Professor Ladon says it's okay for Cassandra to take my place," she told Athena, her words floating above her head. "King Minos's letter specified students, but not necessarily MOA ones. And Professor

Ladon thinks that bringing a non-MOA student is actually a good idea. He said it would increase good feelings between Mount Olympus and Earth if mortals down on Earth hear that a girl who's originally from Troy got invited along." She grinned. "Which I'll make sure they do, of course!"

As Pheme was talking, Eros, who was the godboy of love and had fifth period Revenge-ology with her, came over to join them. "Well, I've decided," he announced. His glittery gold wings fluttered gently, then folded against his back.

He went on, but Athena wasn't listening. She'd been keeping an eye out for Heracles and saw he was now finally exiting the Revenge-ology classroom. Theseus was right behind him, talking away as they passed without even noticing her. She watched the two boys head on down the hallway. She'd only been able to exchange maybe two words with Heracles during fourth period because of that dreadlocked cousin. Ever since his arrival he'd stuck to Heracles like a barnacle on a rock.

"You are such a sweetie," Pheme was saying to Eros. Just tuning back in to their conversation, Athena turned to look at them and caught the smile Eros sent Pheme.

"What did I miss?" she asked the pair.

"I was just telling Pheme I'm going to the journalism conference with her instead of to Crete," he said.

"I'm allowed to bring a guest, so I asked him to come," Pheme explained. "He's interested in journalism too," she added as a pink blush spread across her cheeks.

Why was she blushing? Athena wondered. Did she really think that no one at MOA had figured out that she and Eros were crushing on each other? Ever since Pheme had gotten her wings, she and the also-winged Eros had been spending more and more time together. Athena was glad the two had become such good friends. But why did it seem like whenever you were having boy trouble like she was, other people were always getting along great with their crushes?

Just then Aphrodite, Artemis, and Ares came up the hall. They all had Revenge-ology fifth period too. And behind them were Heracles and Theseus. For some reason they were coming back this way. Athena brightened. Was Heracles returning to talk to her?

As the five of them joined Athena's group standing near the door, Eros followed up on what Pheme had just said. "Yeah, I've been thinking about pitching a relationship advice column to *Teen Scrollazine*. Going to the conference, instead of to Crete, might give me the chance to talk to the staff about it." His chocolate-brown eyes twinkled as he added, "It would be aimed mostly at guys, actually."

Aphrodite's blue eyes blazed with interest. "I've always wanted to see an advice column in the scrollazine, but never had time to write one. Too busy with my Lonely Hearts Club. And I never thought of a guys-only one. What an awesome idea!" she told Eros.

Then she grinned over at Ares, who was standing beside her, and she poked his shoulder lightly with a perfectly pink nail-polished fingertip. "I know of one guy who could definitely use some advice," she teased him.

Ares grinned back at her. "Yeah," he told Eros. "If you need any help with the column, I could give your readers advice about what *not* to do," he joked.

Everyone laughed. Ares and Aphrodite had an

on-again, off-again friendship that had actually been mostly "on" for a while now.

Athena glanced around the group. It seemed like everyone was in like these days, she thought. Aphrodite and Ares. Pheme and Eros. They were only two of the many crushing couples at the Academy. Speaking of which . . . she caught Heracles' eye and smiled at him. It was going to be nice to finally get to hang out with him on the trip to the aMAZEment Park.

Heracles smiled back at her and started to say something. But then Theseus tugged on his arm, and Heracles' attention swung back to him. Athena watched Theseus whisper something in his cousin's ear. "All right. I'll ask," she heard Heracles reply.

"Hey, Eros," he said, clapping a hand on the godboy's shoulder. "Since you're going to a conference, instead of to Crete, can I ask Professor Ladon if my cousin Theseus could take your place?"

"Sure, why not?" Eros said genially.

Oh, great, thought Athena, her heart plummeting. Professor Ladon had thought that inviting non-MOA students was a good idea when Pheme had asked him about letting Cassandra go on the trip. So it was practically a given that he'd agree to taking one more student who didn't attend the Academy. Namely, Theseus, who was now grinning from ear to ear.

"Thanks, godboy dude!" Theseus said to Eros.

"Aren't you expected back in Athens on Friday night?" Athena hinted.

"Yeah," Theseus told her. "But as long as I let my dad know what's up, he'll let me go to the park instead."

Athena couldn't help but think that if Theseus

pestered his father the king as much as he did Heracles, his dad would probably be *glad* to have Theseus gone a while longer. Not that Heracles seemed to object much to the pestering, mind you!

Face it, she told herself. *If you want to spend time with Heracles during the trip, you're also going to be stuck with Theseus.* But, ye gods, how she wished things were different!

4

The Journey

AFTER SCHOOL WAS OUT ON FRIDAY, THE FOUR-teen students going to Crete carried their overnight bags with them and lined up to board an enormous dragon-drawn chariot that had been designed by Professor Ladon.

"Take your placesss insssside in an orderly fassssh-ion!" the professor called out. He was already perched astride the neck of the enormous fierce-looking dragon, prepared to guide it on the upcoming journey. Its bronze and green scales gleamed dully in the afternoon light, and thin streams of fire and smoke puffed from the beast's nostrils when it exhaled.

Though the professor had *some* dragon features— snout, claws, and tail—he stood upright on two feet. The dragon pulling the chariot, however, was the kind that snorted instead of spoke, and it walked on four clawed feet when it wasn't using its wings to fly.

The chariot itself was painted blue and gold, the school colors. The MOA logo and a thunderbolt to represent Zeus were emblazoned on its side. Athena counted seven rows of gold-painted bench seats divided by a center aisle as she boarded behind Heracles and Theseus. Each seat on either side of the aisle was wide enough for two. Unfortunately, as she suspected he would, Theseus grabbed the seat beside Heracles before she even had a *chance* to sit with him.

Wanting to pout, she plopped down in the seat behind the two boys and shoved her bag under her bench. Nearly all of the other students were seating themselves in girl-boy pairs, she noticed: Aphrodite and Ares, Persephone and Hades, Cassandra and Apollo, Medusa and Dionysus. As Artemis and Actaeon boarded the chariot, Athena saw that Artemis wasn't carrying her bow. And no quiver of arrows was strung across her back. It seemed odd to see her without them, but King Minos's letter and Professor Ladon had strictly forbidden weapons.

"Who's taking care of your dogs?" Athena asked as Artemis came even with her seat. Pets weren't allowed on the trip either.

"Iris and Antheia offered to feed and walk them while I'm gone," Artemis replied. Iris was a goddessgirl with a talent for making rainbows, and Antheia was the goddessgirl of flowery wreaths. They were both sweet and liked animals, so Athena wasn't surprised that they'd made the offer.

Pandora was the last student to board. Like the chariot, her hair also matched the school colors. It was gold, with dyed streaks of blue running through it. Athena was relieved when her roommate sat down beside her. It was a good thing that fourteen students had been invited, or she might have wound up sitting alone. How awful—or at least lonely—would that have been?

The dragon unfurled its wide, green-scaled, leathery wings. As its wings began to flap, the chariot lifted off. Pandora peered up through her question-mark-shaped bangs as the chariot soared into the sky, then up and over the peaked roof of the five-story Academy.

"Wow," she said to Athena. "I've never ridden in a chariot pulled by a dragon before, have you?"

Athena was going to say that she hadn't either, but

then Pandora fired off another question. "How long do you think it will take to get to Knossos?"

Knossos was the main city on the island of Crete, where King Minos's palace was located. "I'm not sure, but I think I heard Professor Ladon say it's—" Before Athena could finish saying *a two-hour trip by dragon wing*, Pandora interrupted with two more questions. "Where do you think we'll stay? How many rides do you think there will be in the park?"

That was how conversations often went with Pandora, especially when she was excited. Athena squeezed in a word wherever she could here and there. She also leaned forward just a bit, so she could keep an ear tuned to what Heracles and Theseus were chatting about.

"Which one of your twelve labors was your favorite?" she heard Theseus ask. Ye gods, was he still going on about that hero stuff? she wondered. Still, she found herself holding her breath in anticipation of Heracles' answer.

Would he say it was the first labor they did together? The one in which she'd helped him corral the many-headed Hydra? Or maybe he'd mention the boring Ery-manthian boar. They'd needed to carry the boar off, and she'd had the idea to slip their winged sandals onto his hooves while they rode on his back.

Or maybe he'd choose the last labor she'd helped him complete. The one that had required him to "win the favor of a strong woman." After he'd told her that she was the "strongest woman" he knew, she'd gifted him with the two tapestries she'd woven depicting his labors, thus show-ing he'd won her favor and completed all twelve labors.

She strained to hear as Heracles answered his cousin.

"They were all mega-awesome," he said. "But I think my favorite is either the one where I captured those man-eating horses in Thrace or else maybe the one where I tricked a Geryon so I could steal its herd of red cows."

What? Athena felt like she'd just been punched in the stomach. Heracles had performed those two particular labors alone. She hadn't been with him to help at all!

"Epic!" Theseus exclaimed. "I'd love a chance to battle a Geryon. Or any kind of monster, really. What was it like? Fighting a terrible beast like that?"

"Terrifying," Heracles told him honestly. "It was a typical Geryon—one head, two arms, three bodies, four wings, six legs. Plus vicious talons, slimy green lips, and *extremely* bad breath."

"Worse than a certain professor's?" Theseus asked, shooting a glance at Professor Ladon, where he crouched atop the dragon's long neck ahead of them. The dragon's broad wings flapped rhythmically as the professor guided the chariot onward toward their destination.

Heracles nodded. "Way worse. In fact, its breath was so foul, I nearly passed out a couple of times while facing off with it—even when it was a hundred feet away."

There was a fake, magical Geryon in Professor Ladon's Forest of the Beasts, so Athena knew what they were like. Truly terrifying, like Heracles had said. And the man-eating horses he had battled must have been too. But so were the monsters he and Athena had bested together. She'd given him so much wise counsel during the labors they'd shared. Did picking those other labors as his favorites mean that Heracles hadn't valued her help? And that he liked being on his own more than he liked being with her? She tried not to care. Still, a lump formed in her throat.

Well, she wasn't going to let boy trouble ruin her day. Determinedly she pulled out one of her library scroll-books. It was titled *The History of Farm Implements.*

Eagerly she began reading, hoping to get some inspiration for improvements to her plow.

"Hello?" Pandora said sometime later. She waved a hand in front of Athena's face. "I asked you a question?" she said, as if that were a rare thing for her to do. Which it definitely was not.

"Sorry," said Athena. "What was it again?" She didn't want to admit that she hadn't been listening.

Pandora blew out a puff of air, which fluffed her question-mark-shaped bangs. "I said, how's it going with the plow improvements?"

"Well, as a matter of fact . . ." As Athena began explaining her efforts so far, and the joys and frustrations of invention in general, she started to feel a bit more cheerful. Pandora could actually be a good listener when a subject really interested her. And anything that was related to science, which would include inventions, fascinated her roommate.

A little while later Cassandra announced that she'd brought along a basket of Opposite Oracle-O cookies. This was met with cheers, and her basket was passed around. When each cookie was opened, it spoke its fortune aloud. Athena's fortune said: "You will have a good and bad day."

Huh? Even if you switched her fortune around to the opposite meaning like you were supposed to do with these cookies, it just indicated that she'd have a day that was bad and good, instead of good and bad. Same difference. *Whatever!*

The sun had already begun to set when Professor Ladon shouted back that they were "almossst there." Looking down, Athena could see the outlines of Crete. According to a guidescroll she'd consulted in the MOA library the day before, Crete was Greece's largest island, with a length of one hundred sixty miles and a width of thirty-seven miles.

The city of Knossos was toward the center of the island on the north coast. As the chariot neared it, Athena could see the palace below. It had many multi-floored wings of rooms, built around an inner court-yard, and the palace was surrounded by gardens and fountains except on one side. Near the center of that one side, she spotted what looked like a gigantic set of golden curved bull horns sticking up above the roofline. Since the famous maze ran beneath the palace she guessed that the gigantic golden bull horns marked the entrance to the labyrinth. Below the horns a walkway bordered by red-and-blue-painted columns led straight out from the palace to connect to a magnificent golden archway topped with red and blue flags. The entrance to the aMAZEment Park, of course! Beyond the archway she could see numerous fantastical structures. Those had to be rides and games!

Everyone held on as the teacher dipped the dragon chariot downward, heading for the front of the palace. Athena's hair whipped wildly in the wind. Aphrodite's didn't, she noticed. She'd probably put one of her "don't mess up" spells on it before the trip. It was hard to hear over the wind as they zoomed lower, but when Athena saw Theseus speaking to Heracles, she leaned forward to listen.

"If we *do* come across any monsters while we're on this trip, I'm prepared!" Theseus announced.

Her ears perked up. What did he mean by "prepared"?

Then she heard Heracles give a low whistle. "You shouldn't have brought that," he hissed. "I told you King Minos's invitation said no weapons, remember?"

Athena drew in a sharp breath. Had Theseus brought his dagger—that is, his small *sword*—with him? she wondered, as they landed. That must be it! Well, he'd better keep it hidden if he didn't want to get himself—and possibly Heracles, too—in trouble.

King Minos and his pretty black-haired daughter, Princess Ariadne, greeted the travelers as soon as they stepped from the chariot. Ariadne looked to be about twelve or thirteen, the same age as all fourteen of the visiting students. She wore a cute tiara studded with pink pearls that matched her gown perfectly. Aphrodite immediately complimented her on it before they were even introduced.

"Welcome!" the king boomed out, spreading his arms wide. He wore blue robes and a gold crown. A large man, he had more hair on his chin than on the top of his head. He wasn't as big a guy as Athena's dad, however. Zeus stood nearly seven feet tall!

"I'm so pleased you've come to help celebrate the grand opening of Minos's aMAZEment Park!" the king went on. "You'll have the whole park to yourselves tomorrow. And you're in for a real frightful . . . er, I mean *delightful* experience."

As Professor Ladon and King Minos began discussing arrangements, Athena introduced herself to Princess Ariadne. The girl's lovely hazel eyes went wide with admiration. "OMG!" she exclaimed in a worshipful tone. "You are just, like, sooo inspiring! I mean, wow! Your invention of the sewing arts? Mega-important and . . . and *useful.* I mean, without sewing, we wouldn't have *clothes,*" she bubbled. "And without clothes we'd just be . . . um . . ." As if realizing what she'd been about to say, twin red roses bloomed in her cheeks.

"Well, thanks," Athena said kindly, hoping to lessen her embarrassment.

Ariadne flashed a quick smile. "Just a minute." She flipped her wavy, black hair back over one shoulder as she bent down and pulled something from the sparkly pink bag she was holding. "Ta-da!" she said as she held up a long, pink scarf. It was still attached to knitting needles and a ball of pink yarn, so it obviously wasn't finished yet. She beamed at Athena. "It's my very first knitting project!"

Athena could see at a glance that the girl's stitches were terribly uneven. In places they were way too tight. In others they were too loose. And there were lots of holes in the scarf from dropped stitches.

"Nice pattern," Athena said, studying it. After all, Ariadne was clearly excited about her project, and Athena didn't want to hurt her feelings. Then, giving Ariadne a thumbs-up, she added, "Good job!"

"Thanks," said Ariadne. "That means a lot, coming from you."

"Follow me to the palace!" King Minos called out.

"Dooms . . . I mean *rooms* are ready for all of you in the east wing!"

Athena wondered if he always had trouble mixing up his words like that. Students hoisted their bags and began to follow the king and Professor Ladon toward the huge two-story, multi-winged stone palace.

Ariadne handed her knitting bag to a servant and then fell into step beside Athena just as Aphrodite came up on Athena's other side. "Heracles and Theseus sure are as thick as thieves. And look at that silly Ares," Aphrodite remarked to Athena while glancing over her shoulder.

Athena looked back too. As usual, all the guys were deep in conversation. Ares, who was the godboy of war, was pretending to thrust an invisible sword into an invisible opponent. And from the motions the rest of them were making as they talked—slicing their hands across their throats and punching the air with their fists—

she guessed it was more talk about fighting and hero-ism. Godsamighty! Didn't they have anything better to discuss?

"I'd hoped to spend some time with Heracles on this trip," Athena confessed to Aphrodite wistfully. "But with Theseus here—"

"Which one is he?" interrupted Ariadne, also glancing back.

After flashing Athena a crafty smile, Aphrodite looked over at Ariadne. "He's Heracles' cousin. The cute guy with the dreadlocks," she replied.

"Ooh. He really *is* cute," Ariadne agreed.

Not as cute as Heracles, thought Athena. But she didn't say so, of course.

Aphrodite leaned forward a little as the three girls continued to walk, so she could speak to Ariadne more easily. "Know something?" Aphrodite told her. "I just realized that you and Theseus have a lot in common. I mean, your fathers are both kings. Your mothers are queens. You're a princess. He's a prince. And, well, I could go on and on about all the other things you have in common, but why don't I just introduce him to you? Then you can find out for yourself."

"Oh. My. Godz. Could you?" Ariadne practically squealed in delight, clapping her hands. "That would be, like, sooo awesome!"

Athena hid a smile behind one hand. As the goddess-girl of love, Aphrodite was mega-good at matchmaking.

By now they'd almost reached the palace doors. They slowed a little, and Aphrodite looked over her shoulder, crooking a finger at Theseus behind them. "Could you come here a minute?" she called out to him.

Since few boys ever refused Aphrodite anything—they were *that* mesmerized by her great beauty—Theseus trotted over obediently to see what she wanted.

Aphrodite nudged Ariadne to Theseus's side, and at the same time she gave Athena a little shove in Heracles' direction. "Now's your chance," she whispered to Athena.

Not only was she trying to help the princess, but she had obviously realized Athena was missing Heracles and was trying to help her, too. As the goddess of love, she really was good at sniffing out relationships that had potential—as well as troubled ones!

However, before Athena could reach Heracles' side, a teenage boy with short, dark hair and ears that stuck out from his head burst through the palace doors and came toward her. It was the inventor/architect Daedalus. She recognized him from a drawing she'd seen in the *Greekly Weekly News*. He must have recognized her, too, because a big smile spread over his face. He strode right up to her.

Athena was just about to introduce herself and tell him

how excited she was to meet him, when he spoke to her first. "Athena!" he gushed. "I've been dying to meet you!"

Huh? He had?

"To tell you I think your inventions are brilliant! Perfection, in fact," he continued enthusiastically.

"Well, thanks," she replied, feeling flattered. Ever since she'd found out she was an immortal that day when Zeus had first invited her to attend MOA, she'd become used to mortals being in awe of her. Still, she wasn't *perfect*. But with Heracles ignoring her lately, Daedalus's obvious admiration puffed up her wounded pride. It was nice to have another inventor think so highly of her work.

"Of course, the very best of my inventions pale by comparison to the very least of yours," Daedalus continued. "But, well, I was wondering if you maybe, might possibly, perhaps be willing to come take a look at the labyrinth I built anyway?"

"You mean now?" Athena asked. She darted a glance at Heracles, who was busy straightening his lion cape. She'd so wanted to hang out with him, and this was her first chance to do so without Theseus around. But she'd also wanted to talk to Daedalus, inventor to inventor. What if another opportunity for that didn't come along on this trip?

"Yes, I'd really like your opinion on it before it publicly opens tomorrow." Daedalus followed her gaze to Heracles, and his eyes widened a little nervously. The sight of the lion cape sometimes had that effect on mortals. "Um, if that's okay," he added.

"Wow! Thanks for the offer," Athena hedged, stalling for time. The labyrinth was the star attraction of the funpark. It was why King Minos had named it Minos's aMAZEment Park. So naturally Athena wanted a preview! She glanced back at Heracles again, feeling torn.

Catching her eye, he smiled and headed her way.

"Could Heracles come too?" Athena asked Daedalus quickly.

"Come where?" asked Heracles as he joined them. Seeming a little distracted, he glanced toward Theseus while awaiting a reply, as if to make sure his cousin was okay. Theseus was chatting enthusiastically with Ariadne as Aphrodite looked on approvingly, but he darted Heracles a look too, and waved.

"To see the labyrinth," Athena told Heracles. She moved her head into his line of vision to get his attention. "Daedalus offered me a sneak peek before it opens tomorrow."

"Cool. You should go, then," Heracles told her. "I'll keep an eye on . . . I mean, wait up for Theseus."

"Oh. Are you sure?" Athena asked, feeling disappointed. She looked at Daedalus. "You're okay with

Heracles coming too, right?" she added, hoping Heracles might change his mind.

"Sure," said Daedalus.

Heracles shook his head, causing the gaping lion hood of his cape to bob a little. Daedalus gave the lion head a nervous look and took a step backward. "That's okay," Heracles replied. "You'll probably have a bunch of invention stuff to talk about, and I'd only be in the way. Catch you later?"

Athena nodded, though she really felt a little troubled by his response. Well, she guessed she knew where she rated in her crush's affections. Right *behind* his cousin!

"This way," Daedalus said. His big ears wiggled with excitement as he pointed toward the side of the palace where Athena had earlier glimpsed the golden bull horns at the labyrinth's entrance.

Disappointed that Heracles had chosen not to come

with them, but still anxious to see the labyrinth, Athena picked up her overnight bag and started to follow the inventor.

"Athena, wait!" Heracles called to her after she'd only gone a few steps.

Her heart lifted. Had he changed his mind and decided to come after all?

No such luck. Instead all he said was, "While you go to the maze I'll take your bag for you and make sure it gets put in whatever room you'll be staying in."

"Okay, thanks," she said as he hurried over to take her overnight bag. It was really heavy, especially since she didn't travel anywhere without packing several scroll-books. You never knew when you might get free time, so she thought it wise to keep something to read handy.

Heracles lifted her bag as easily as if it weighed less than a quill pen. He was so incredibly strong! It *was* nice of him to take her bag, just as it was nice of him to shepherd Theseus around. She sighed, suddenly realizing she hadn't been being fair to him. Of course he'd want to hang out with Theseus. He didn't often get the chance. From now on she'd try to be more considerate, just as he was being right now, she promised herself.

As Heracles turned and walked away with her bag hefted over one shoulder, Athena ran to catch up with Daedalus. Her decision made, new excitement filled her. How special that she would be first to get a peek at this labyrinth!

5

The Labyrinth

ATHENA ROUNDED THE SIDE OF THE PALACE. UP ahead she could see the columned walkway, which she judged to be about thirty feet long. On the far right end of it was the golden archway entrance to the aMAZEment Park with all the red and blue flags. At the far left end of the walkway was the palace wall with a red door and the golden horns.

Even from a distance she could see that the funpark

archway entrance was carved and brightly painted with the name of the park and fanciful depictions of various monsters, creatures, heroes, and gods featured in the rides and games. She'd read in the *Greekly Weekly News* that several of the rides and games in the park were modeled on events that had taken place during Odysseus's journey home to Ithaca. It thrilled her that the hero *she* had mentored had inspired parts of Daedalus's a-*maze*-ing creation.

She finally caught up with the teenage inventor before the bright red door. It was huge, with golden hinges set in the wall. Directly above it loomed the golden lintel top, carved in the shape of a bull's bigger-than-life horns.

"Wow, fancy," Athena remarked with a grin.

"It's part of the park theme," said Daedalus, nodding. "Horns. You know, like the Minotaur's."

Athena nodded. After passing through the bright red door, they went down a long flight of stone stairs. The stairs ended in a round room with light brown walls and a cement floor with a patterned dark brown decorative border running around it. "So the maze is down here?" she asked, looking around.

"We're under the palace now," replied Daedalus. He pointed ahead to three arched openings in the room's circular wall. "Those are three possible entrances to the labyrinth. Each will lead visitors along a different path in the maze."

"Their goal? To reach the middle of the maze, where the dreaded Minotaur awaits," Athena supplied in a dramatic voice that made him laugh.

"Exactly! Of course the paths connect and separate throughout the labyrinth, so visitors can meet up or go different directions now and then. Depending on which way they think will get them there fastest," Daedalus explained. Then he gestured toward the three entrances. "Your pick."

Athena grinned and headed for the center entrance. "This one," she said, and he followed her in.

Beyond the arched opening, they entered a tunnel—the start of the labyrinth. She was bouncing with excitement to test her skill at puzzle-solving. Would she be able to find her way to the center on her own? She studied their surroundings carefully to avoid getting lost on the way in and so she'd be able to find her way out later. She didn't want to have to ask for help with directions unless it was absolutely necessary.

"I thought it would be dark inside this labyrinth, since it's so cavelike and since it's under the palace," Athena commented. "Those were a good idea," she added, gesturing at the torches that jutted out from the tunnel's walls every ten feet or so. By the golden light they gave off, she could see that many of the walls had been artfully decorated with frescoes—murals showing scenes of bull-leaping contests, and people dancing and feasting. "Beautiful," she murmured, running her hand along the fresco to her left. "I've never seen such deep, rich reds and blues."

Daedalus preened, obviously pleased by her praise. "I hired the finest artists and builders in Crete. The frescoes will give visitors something to look at while they're trying to find their way to the center of the maze and then back out again."

"Are they location clues, too?" she guessed. He nodded, his eyes sparkling.

The passage they followed twisted and turned, and its floor was studded with fake stalagmites that you had to be careful not to stumble over. However, to her disappointment, it wasn't really all that hard to navigate, she soon began to realize. And there were only a few, short dead ends angling off the main path to add interest and to make you backtrack. *Hmm.*

"Are any of the three main paths more challenging than the others?" she asked him hopefully.

He nodded, and relief filled her. But it quickly fled when he added, "This one is the hardest."

Huh? That was bad news, she thought. She crossed her fingers that the maze would get harder later on. Surely it would. Daedalus knew what he was doing. Right?

"The number and variety of your inventions is astounding," Daedalus remarked enthusiastically, picking up their earlier conversation as they rounded a corner along the path. "From musical instruments to math, the olive, the sewing arts, ships, and chariots. I mean, the list goes on and on."

"Well, there are just so many things that interest me," Athena said modestly as she stepped over a stalagmite that had been painted with red and blue polka dots. "I bet you're the same way." She welcomed the chance to chat, since the maze unfortunately wasn't really keeping her brain occupied.

Daedalus shook his head. "Not really. My inventions are mostly limited to architectural and mechanical things. I don't know how you do it. I wish I possessed one tenth of your creative ability!"

Though Athena felt a bit embarrassed by his over-the-top flattery, it also made her feel pretty good. She was a goddess, after all. Being worshipped by mortals was part of the package! Daedalus's praise boosted her feelings of pride in her inventions. And her confidence, too. Did Heracles feel a similar boost in his pride and confidence when Theseus praised his heroics? she wondered. Probably so. Realizing this made her feel more understanding of how he'd been acting since Theseus had arrived.

As they approached the center of the labyrinth, the twists and turns came faster, but there were fewer trick dead ends to trip her up. Along the way Athena couldn't help imagining ways the labyrinth's design could be improved to make it more complex. Right now it was really so simple that anyone could easily find their way out of it just by keeping one hand on a wall and following it to the center and then back out again. So, although it was beautiful, it wasn't exactly . . . fun.

Eventually they came to a six-sided room painted blood-red that was about twice the size of the dorm room she shared with Pandora back at the Academy. Athena stopped cold and gasped at the sight that met them.

"Behold the vicious Minotaur!" Daedalus crowed, gesturing toward it with the sweep of his arm.

The mechanical monster he'd created stood at the center of the hexagonal room and was fantastic! It had the body of a man and the head and tail of a bull. The gold ring through its nose gleamed in the light of the torches lining the room. Its eyes seemed to stare at her fiercely. She took a step back, her own gray-blue eyes going wide. Then she paused.

"Why isn't it moving?" she whispered.

"Don't worry. It's not turned on right now," he said, which instantly relaxed her.

"Sorry," she said sheepishly. "But that thing scared me for a second. It's almost an exact replica of the Minotaurs in the Forest of the Beasts! Same humongous size. Bull horns, two clawed hands, two hooved feet. Same menacing look in its red eyes." She shivered.

"Does that mean you like it?" he teased. "Here, come look closer." He drew her to the center of the room toward the Minotaur. Still, she held back a little and didn't venture too near it.

As she studied the mechanical beast, Daedalus watched eagerly. "So you've been through my maze. Give me your honest opinion. I'm dying to know what you think."

"Well, I think this Minotaur is *super*-scary. That is to say, a-*maze*-ing!" she said after a moment, which made him smile. "So lifelike." She purposely avoided sharing her misgivings about the labyrinth itself. She didn't want to dim his enthusiasm for the field of invention or hurt his feelings. Yet she didn't want to lie, either. So she didn't point out what she saw as the labyrinth's biggest flaw— that it was way too easy!

Luckily, Daedalus didn't seem to notice her lack of enthusiasm. "I'm so glad you like it," he said, sounding pleased. "The Minotaur looks even scarier when it's turned on. But don't worry. I made it so it can't move more than a few steps in any direction."

"Can I see? I mean, could you turn it on for a few seconds, maybe?" Athena asked, thinking there must be an on-off switch on the monster somewhere.

Daedalus shook his head. "Sorry. I would if I could. But the controls that operate it are in my workshop upstairs." He pointed up, and she glanced in that direction to see that the ceiling overhead was made of thick, opaque glass. "It's one-way glass. Visitors down here can't see me in the control room, but from up there I can look down and see them. That way I can keep tabs on what's going on. So if anyone gets scared or the Minotaur malfunctions, I can use the speaker system to calm everyone, and use the controls to turn this monster off. I wish I could see the whole maze though. I hope no one gets too terribly lost, because I won't be able to guide them out."

"Oh, yeah, that's too bad," Athena said, nodding. She didn't tell him not to worry. That his maze was so easy that no one could ever get lost in here, except maybe a two-year-old. Instead she said, "Well, I bet your Minotaur will send shivers down everyone's spines when they see it tomorrow." Though she tried to sound super-enthusiastic, she was concerned that when the maze was revealed tomorrow, it was going to be a flop. It had only taken ten minutes or so to reach the Minotaur, and they'd been walking at a pretty leisurely pace.

Should she tell her friends ahead of time what to expect and warn them to be supportive? she wondered as they left the Minotaur room and headed back through the maze. Regardless, once other visitors came later on, word was bound to get back to Daedalus and King Minos that this labyrinth—which was supposed to be the grand centerpiece of the amusement park—was actually pretty lame. Daedalus's feelings were sure to be hurt. Worse, it was just possible that Minos might fire him, and that would be awful!

"Don't give away any secrets about what you've seen, okay?" Daedalus cautioned her as they left the labyrinth through the red door. "We don't want to ruin the thrills and surprises in store for everyone tomorrow. I can't wait to see how much fun your friends have trying to figure out the puzzle. If they like the maze as much as you do, buzz will spread. It will become famous!"

"That truly would be a-*maze*-ing," Athena told him. He laughed, but she'd actually been half-joking. Because she *would* be amazed if the praise and fame he hoped for came to pass once visitors saw how boring the labyrinth was. Should she warn him? Before she could decide, they ran into other students from MOA sightseeing on the palace grounds, and Daedalus bade her farewell. As

Athena watched him go, she couldn't help feeling that the guy was in for a disappointing reaction tomorrow. But still, she would hope for the best.

That night, there was a lavish dinner in the palace's Banquet Hall in honor of the visiting students. There were even more frescoes here than in the labyrinth, and the floor was beautifully tiled with mosaics. Bordered by a geometric pattern of red lines, painted blue dolphins frolicked in ocean waves along all four sides of the Hall, which was brightly lit by torches.

In the center of the hall, between red-painted columns, the girls all sat on pillow-topped benches clustered around one long table, and the boys all sat at another. Athena had worn her best blue chiton with a scalloped hem for the occasion and had wound gold and blue ribbons through her long wavy brown hair. Aphrodite wore pink and red, her hair topped by the cutest silver tiara set with red rubies. Persephone's chiton was flowy and green, and Artemis had decided on a gold one. Aphrodite had helped her fashion her dark hair into a dramatic twist that had a small golden arrow decoration sticking through it. It was so adorable!

King Minos and Professor Ladon sat at another table at the front of the room together. Musicians played lutes nearby, and jugglers performed, tossing knives and flaming torches for everyone's entertainment.

Glinting in the torchlight, gold and silver serving dishes were piled high with all kinds of delicious things to eat. There were enormous platters of roasted chicken; bunches of luscious purple grapes; hummus made from chickpeas; bread and honey; and huge bowls of leafy green salad with cucumbers, dill, and—perhaps as a tribute to Athena—*olives.*

As they sat eating, Athena and her friends compared

notes about the various things they'd seen and done since their arrival. Because the aMAZEment Park wasn't open until tomorrow, mostly they'd spent their time wandering through the various wings of the palace or out in the courtyard at the palace's center. Athena had done some sketches of a large, dramatic outdoor water fountain that she planned to show Poseidon upon her return to the Academy.

"Isn't it great that all of our bedrooms are on the ground floor and open up into the courtyard?" Persephone said excitedly. "It'll be like sleeping in the middle of a garden!"

Athena smiled at her enthusiasm as she helped herself to some grapes.

"No surprise that the goddessgirl of spring and growing things would be so excited about our sleeping arrangements," Aphrodite noted in amusement.

Athena had gotten a quick peek at her own room after

she and her friends had returned to the main rooms of the palace before dinner. Aphrodite's and her names had been written in calligraphy on a papyrus card on the door of the room they were to share. And thanks to Heracles her bag had been sitting on the floor next to one of the two canopy beds draped in white satin.

The room had ocean-blue walls with a wavelike painted decorative border. And there were a half dozen matching blue pillows with white tassels atop the beds. A white wardrobe and a makeup table were the only other pieces of furniture in the small, tidy room. As Persephone had noted, big double doors in all of their rooms opened into the large central courtyard, which was filled with beautiful flowers and fountains.

"Can you believe we get to be the very first visitors to go on the rides and explore the labyrinth tomorrow? I can hardly wait!" Artemis exclaimed.

Hearing her reference to the labyrinth, Athena snapped to attention. She frowned inwardly as Artemis speared a potato and dropped it onto her plate.

Medusa looked across the table at Athena. "You saw the labyrinth, right?" she asked as she tossed twelve grapes into the air. *Snap! Snap!* Each of the dozen snakes that grew from her head grabbed one and swallowed it down. MOA students had grown used to her snakes snacking like this. However, Ariadne observed it with startled eyes.

"Yeah, when Heracles brought your bag to our room, he said Daedalus was taking you on a preview tour," Aphrodite added.

Athena nodded as she spread butter on a piece of bread. "Yes, I saw it."

"And?" asked Artemis, her fork poised halfway between her plate and her mouth.

Athena glanced at Ariadne. She was sitting between Aphrodite and Pandora. Until this moment Pandora had been peppering the princess with questions, but now all of the girls at the table were looking at Athena. Cassandra and Medusa included.

Athena gulped, then said brightly, "It was interesting."

Persephone cocked her head. "Interesting how?"

"Oh, you know," Athena said vaguely. "Lots of twists and turns."

Artemis frowned with disappointment. "Is that all?"

"No! Of course not!" Athena said, aware of Ariadne's eyes on her. She wished she knew what the girl was thinking. Had *she* seen the labyrinth yet and formed an opinion? If so, she wasn't saying.

Cassandra's almond-shaped brown eyes lit up as she smiled. "I'm guessing Athena doesn't want to give away any surprises." She glanced at her. "Am I right?"

If that was a prediction, it definitely wasn't one of her better ones, thought Athena. But she nodded anyway. She only hoped that her friends' expectations for the labyrinth wouldn't be completely dashed when they actually went through it tomorrow. Poor Daedalus!

"Oof. I'm sooo stuffed!" Ariadne said. She pushed her plate away, and then she reached down for her sparkly pink bag and pulled out her knitting.

Athena approved of her devotion to knitting and often knitted at lunch back at MOA herself. However, to Athena's skilled eye, the lumpy pink scarf looked way too long already. Apparently Ariadne didn't think so, since she just kept going on it. As her needles clicked together, she glanced over at the boys' table. The boys were talking to one of the jugglers and admiring his knives.

"Theseus is really interested in weaponry," Ariadne

noted. "When he told me that, I was like, wow, really? 'Cause my dad's got an awesome collection of swords, bows, helmets, and shields." She paused, then looked up from her knitting. "Do you think maybe I should ask Theseus if he wants to see them?"

Aphrodite and Athena exchanged a knowing look. For some unfathomable reason (unfathomable to Athena, anyway) Ariadne had fallen for Heracles' cousin! Was the feeling mutual, though? Theseus seemed way too obsessed with becoming a hero to have any leftover attention to lavish on a crush. Even one as pretty and sweet (though somewhat bubble-headed, perhaps) as Ariadne.

"You definitely should ask him," Aphrodite said.

"But only if your dad's collection is securely locked up," Athena added, only half-joking.

When dinner was over, a grand entertainment with

more jugglers, musicians, gymnasts, and actors began. The jugglers were really good, but even as they tossed flaming torches back and forth, Athena couldn't stop worrying about tomorrow's grand opening of the labyrinth. Would it bomb horribly? It was too bad, really, because with a few small improvements the labyrinth could be so much better.

While the others watched the entertainment, her head began to spin with ideas. Changes she'd have made if she'd been the one to design the maze. The walls needed rearranging, for one thing. And while the stalagmites were nice, why not add stalactites, too!

As ideas came and went in her mind, she got more and more excited. And fidgety. She couldn't just stand by and watch the labyrinth Daedalus had worked so hard on flop.

At last, convinced that he required her help whether

he knew it or not, Athena sneaked away from the table. After grabbing a torch from a wall sconce, she made her way out. Once outside the palace, she went around it till she reached the red door topped with the lintel of bull horns. And after slipping inside the door, she sped downstairs.

6
Making Improvements

Friday Night

Luckily the torches were still lit in the brown room at the bottom of the stairs, because Athena's one torch wouldn't have been enough to light her way. Probably the torches were kept lit day and night, she guessed as she passed through the center arch again. She placed one hand against a wall and kept it there as she went straight to the center of the labyrinth, only pausing briefly to dodge or hop over the brightly colored stalagmites that jutted up from the cement floor.

Even though the mechanical Minotaur was in exactly the same position as when she'd seen it earlier—it couldn't have moved, since it was turned off—its fierceness startled her yet again as she came upon it.

She wagged a finger at it. "Yeah, you do look pretty terrifying. But stop scaring me, okay?" For a few seconds she broke into giggles at her silliness. Then it was time to get serious. She had work to do.

Starting here at the center of the labyrinth, Athena hurried back through it, pausing here and there to chant a series of "complex" spells she'd learned at the Academy that would break apart the labyrinth walls to create a far more complex maze. They began:

"Walls, split and move about.

Make it harder to get out."

While chanting the spells, she aimed a finger at various sections along the corridor walls. *Crack! Rumble. Rumble.* The places she pointed to immediately split off from the whole like calving glaciers. She hopped out of the way as the newly created pieces of wall moved to different positions. Some stayed disconnected and freestanding, while others joined together with pieces to form new angles, turns, and dead ends. She left the frescoed walls intact, however, not wanting to ruin the beautiful wall paintings.

Now and then she cast other spells along the way to cause stalactites to hang down from above for more color and artistic decoration:

"Come, stalactites, bright and appealing.

Grow like icicles from the ceiling."

She smiled with satisfaction as the brightly colored, striped, and polka-dotted stalactites appeared overhead. When she'd been younger, she'd sometimes gotten stalagmites and stalactites confused. But then she'd created an easy way to tell them apart. "Stalactite" contained the letter *C* for "ceiling," which was where stalactites formed. And "stalagmite" contained the letter *G* for "ground," which was where stalagmites grew. After she'd figured that out, remembering which formation was which had become easy-peasy.

If she'd had more time, she would've made additional improvements. Added more monsters, for example. But creating a monster was a much more complicated task than splitting up and moving walls or growing a bunch of stalactites.

Besides, it wouldn't be fair to upstage Daedalus's mechanical Minotaur. It was truly fantastic, and Athena was sure he'd worked hard on it. So instead she contented herself with creating a dozen ghoulishly grinning stone gargoyles to gaze down at her fellow students as they wandered through the maze.

She knew she'd done a good job of making the labyrinth trickier to navigate when she got turned around a couple of times on her way back out and ended up having to retrace her steps. Yes! Success!

Once she was finally back in the round room facing the three arched entrances to the labyrinth, she knew she didn't have time to go up and down the other two tunnels. She'd soon be missed at dinner. So she quickly cast spells from where she stood, sending magic down the first and third tunnels to alter them in ways similar to—and yet different from—how she'd changed the middle one.

When she was done, a feeling of pride spread through her. She'd tweaked Daedalus's simple maze into a complex one that would be much more difficult and therefore lots more fun. Her improvements were sure to turn his formerly boring labyrinth into a *real* star attraction!

After running up the flight of stairs she'd gone down earlier, Athena pushed through the red door to the outside. Then she hurried back around the palace and made her way to the entrance to the banquet hall to rejoin the dinner party.

She saw at once that the pillow-topped benches they'd sat on at dinner had been moved from the tables to form an arc closer to the entertainers. Some students had traded places to sit next to their crushes. And everyone on the benches was so engrossed in the mock battle scene now being staged between four actors that no one seemed to notice as Athena took a seat on the far end of a bench.

Except Ariadne, that is. The black-haired princess eyed her curiously, then smiled and pointed to a costumed "monster" that had just entered through a door near the makeshift stage. The front half of the monster resembled a horse, but its back half sported the wings and tail feathers of a rooster.

"It's a Hippalectryon!" Athena heard Artemis exclaim to her crush, Actaeon. Athena recognized it too, as one of the many beasts Professor Ladon had lectured about in Beast-ology class.

The Hippalectryon tossed its head and snorted as it wobbled toward the four battling actors, who were dressed as soldiers. It flapped its wings and strutted around in such a silly way that she and the others giggled. From the

way the goofy monster moved, plus the two pairs of sandaled feet sticking out from beneath it, Athena could tell
that there were two actors inside the costume, one standing in front of the other.

Until now the battling soldier-actors had pretended
not to notice the Hippalectryon. But as she watched, it
went up to one of the soldiers and nudged him with its
long horse snout. The soldier-actor gave a hysterical mock
shriek and jumped into the arms of one of his friends.
Then the pair of them ran off, disappearing through
the same door through which the Hippalectryon had
appeared just minutes before.

As Athena and the rest of the audience laughed, she
glanced around the room for Heracles. Though there
was a ring of torches around the area where the actors
were performing, the seating area was shadowy. She
couldn't see him, which was too bad. She would've liked

to go sit with him, so they could enjoy this show together.

When laughter rang out from the audience around her again, Athena's attention swung back to the mock battle. There were only two soldiers left onstage now, and the Hippalectryon was sitting on one of them. It was tickling him with its tail feathers. Meanwhile, the other soldier sneaked up behind the monster and pretended to poke it in the behind with his sword. With a loud whinny the Hippalectryon leaped clumsily into the air. The soldier that had been beneath him rolled away from the monster and jumped to his feet. Miming terror, he too raced for the exit, causing giggles and chuckles to fill the room.

Now the Hippalectryon began to chase the sole remaining soldier around and around in circles till at last the soldier turned on it. *Whomp!* He brought his sword down, "slicing" the monster in two so that the front horse half split off from the back rooster half. The two halves fell to the floor, shuddered a few moments, and then lay still. The victorious soldier waved his sword over his head and then bowed to the cheers of the audience.

Grinning and clapping along with everyone else, Athena craned her neck, looking for Heracles again. She was hoping to catch his eye so they could share a laugh across the crowd. As before, Ariadne looked her way and smiled. She cocked her head toward the vanquished Hippalectryon lying on the floor.

Athena raised her eyebrows and shoulders, sending her a questioning look. By now the soldiers who had run off had returned to the makeshift stage to take a few bows. They gestured to the slain Hippalectryon at their feet. Suddenly the two halves of the monster came back to life. Jumping up, the actors inside threw off the pieces of their costume.

Athena's mouth fell open in surprise. The actors inside were none other than Heracles and Theseus! That must've been what Ariadne had been trying to tell her all along with her gestures toward the monster.

Now Heracles kicked his horse's head out of the way, and Theseus plucked a tail feather from his dreadlocks. They both bowed as the audience roared and clapped and whistled its approval.

Athena leaned over to whisper to Aphrodite. "I stepped outside for a minute. How did Heracles and Theseus end up onstage?"

"The actors asked for volunteers from the audience to play the part of the monster," Aphrodite whispered back. "Weren't they great?"

"Fantastic," Athena enthused, clapping along with everyone else.

Once Heracles and Theseus had finished their bows,

the real actors invited the rest of the students to come forward to check out the monster costume and other props. Ares was the first to take up the invitation. He was soon followed by most of the audience, including Athena and Ariadne.

Ares slipped the horse half of the costume over his head and then struck a pose. "How do I look?" he asked.

"Ha! A horse's *rear* end would suit you better," quipped Apollo. The two boys started trading joking insults, and some of the others joined in.

"You were, like, soo terrific!" Ariadne exclaimed to Theseus as she drew near.

"Oh, thanks," he replied a little bashfully. Then he seemed to notice Actaeon, who was examining one of the soldier's swords.

Without another word to the princess, Theseus darted over to Actaeon. "Do you like swords?" Athena heard

Theseus say to him. "Because if you do, I have an amazing one. My dad gave it to me. Want to see—" He reached toward his hip.

Suddenly Heracles came barreling toward him. He didn't even seem to notice Athena as he brushed past her and ran smack-dab into his cousin. On purpose, she was sure.

Oomph! Theseus was knocked aside. With an apologetic glance at Actaeon, Heracles grabbed his cousin's arm and began tugging him toward the rooms where the boys would be sleeping. "We'd better get going. Need to get up early so we'll have lots of time to enjoy the rides, right?"

Looking a little dizzy, Theseus just mumbled, "Um, uh, yeah."

As Heracles rushed his cousin away, Athena saw her crush whisper urgently into the other boy's ear. Heracles seemed mad. No doubt he was scolding Theseus. Professor

Ladon had been talking to King Minos only a short distance away when the boy had tried to show his dagger . . . er . . . *sword* to Actaeon. Theseus would probably have gotten sent home to Athens pronto if King Minos or Professor Ladon had found out he'd brought it.

"Sooo, I guess I'll see you tomorrow, then, huh?" Ariadne called to Theseus as he and Heracles passed by. Neither boy took any notice of her.

Poor girl, thought Athena. She had about as much chance of snagging Theseus's attention right now as Athena had of snagging Heracles'. Which was to say, not much. She could only hope that tomorrow would be different. For the princess and for her!

7

Trapped!

AS BREAKFAST ENDED IN THE BANQUET HALL the next morning, King Minos appeared. He was dressed in ceremonial garb, with a purple cloak slung over his fine linen tunic. A gold-leaf crown sat atop his almost bald head.

"Ladies and Gentlemen," he called out in a grand and theatrical style that befitted a circus ringmaster. "Are you all feeling fearful—I mean *cheerful*—about today's grand opening of Minos's aMAZEment Park?" He paused as his fourteen young guests shouted out "Yes!" and applauded and cheered enthusiastically.

He beamed at them. "Thank you very much! I'm pleased to hear it. We will be saving the beast—ahem . . . the *best* till last. The a-*maze*-ing labyrinth with our star attraction—its Minotaur—will open at exactly noon. However, all other rides and games are now open for your enjoyment. So *go*," he urged them. "And have fun!"

The students didn't need to be told twice. There was practically a stampede as everyone jumped up from the dining tables and stormed toward the exit doors.

Athena, Aphrodite, Persephone, and Artemis moved off together. But once they were outside, heading around the side of the palace toward the walkway and the tall arched golden entrance to the funpark, people started pairing off. Just ahead of her, walking hand in hand now, were Aphrodite and Ares, Artemis and Actaeon, Persephone and Hades, Apollo and Cassandra, and Medusa and Dionysus. Pandora was following Professor Ladon, asking a million questions.

Athena wished she could catch up with Heracles. However, he and Theseus were already way too far ahead. She'd only just rounded the side of the palace when she saw them pass between two columns of the walkway and then veer right under the grand golden entrance arch with its waving flags and paintings of monsters, creatures, heroes, and gods.

She looked around for Daedalus, thinking maybe they could hang out. In fact, maybe she should have let him know about the changes she'd made in his maze before now, she realized. But he was nowhere in sight.

Which left Athena alone. *Great.* Alone was so *not* the way to enjoy a funpark!

After passing under the golden arch, Athena saw a ride called the Shipwreck off to her left. A half dozen ships that were actually rides modeled after the ships that Odysseus and his men had sailed were lined up in a trough of water. Each ship could seat four people and was waiting to sail into a dark tunnel that would presumably lead visitors through simulated terrors like the ones Odysseus and his men had encountered.

Aphrodite came up beside her, her blue eyes twinkling with excitement. "Want to go on it with me?"

"Sure," said Athena. She looked around. "But where's Ares?"

Aphrodite motioned toward the far end of the aMAZEment Park. "He and a bunch of the guys wanted to try out the bumper chariots first. I told him I'd catch him later."

"But don't you want to go on the bumper chariots

with him?" Athena asked. It had crossed her mind that Aphrodite might have noticed her standing alone and felt sorry for her. Was that the real reason she'd offered her company? Not that it wasn't nice of her, but Athena didn't want to be pitied.

"Nuh-uh," Aphrodite replied. "Remember how Pheme had all that trouble with that boy, Phaeton, who sneaked into MOA a while back? The one who drove Helios's chariot too close to the sun? Well, that's the theme of the bumper chariots. Flames and terror. It would probably melt my makeup off and singe my hair. Uh, no thanks!" She gave her long, stylish golden hair a fluff.

Artemis and Persephone overheard as they came along to join them. "Yeah, we decided to skip the bumper chariots for now too," Persephone said to Aphrodite. "This ship ride looks like way more fun."

"I do want to try the bumper chariots later, though," said Artemis. "So I can tell Pheme about them."

Athena smiled at her friends, relieved that she wouldn't have to tour the park alone after all. Also, it seemed unlikely that all three of her GGBFFs had purposely ditched their guys for her sake. But if they had . . . well, she would just feel honored and go with it. Hanging out with her favorite goddessgirl friends was a great way to start things off.

All four girls piled into one of the ships. Aphrodite and Athena sat on the bench seat in front, while Persephone and Artemis sat behind them.

As soon as they were settled, their ship gave a jerk and began to move forward through the water trough as if blown ahead by a strong wind. They entered the tunnel, which was lit with flaming torches every few feet. Soon the goddessgirls heard singing. Incredibly beautiful singing that made them really want to get closer to hear it better. Rounding a corner, they came upon the source: three mechanical women perched on a jagged rock to their right.

"Sirens!" Athena exclaimed.

"Their music is enchanted," said Aphrodite.

"Meant to lure us to our doom!" added Artemis.

Still singing, the Sirens' hands reached out toward the girls as if imploring them to sail closer. "Nuh-uh," said Persephone, holding her fists over her ears. "Not going to happen." But then, without warning, their ship lurched toward the rocks. *Splash!* A spray of water almost got them. The girls screamed, and then laughed with relief as their ship slipped past the rock and sailed on.

Next they encountered a mechanical representation of Scylla. The sea monster's tentacle-like legs slapped the water as the mouth in each of its six heads snapped open and shut, revealing rows of sharp-looking teeth.

"No! Get away!" yelled Aphrodite, her blue eyes rounding.

"Eek!" yelled Athena. She wasn't truly scared, but the sea monster *was* a frightening sight, and it was fun pretending to be terrified with her friends. Just as it seemed the girls would be swallowed up by one of Scylla's heads, their ship lurched sideways.

"Phew. Glad that's over," said Artemis. However, when their ship suddenly began to whirl around in circles, she added, "Oops. Guess I spoke too soon." The girls shrieked as they clung to the sides of their little ship. It felt like they were about to be sucked down into the depths of Charybdis, a giant whirlpool.

Abruptly their ship stopped spinning and tacked toward Scylla again. "Oh, great," said Persephone. "Looks

126

like we'll be chomped to bits after all." At the last moment, however, their ship veered back on track.

As the ride continued on, the girls passed through a vicious-sounding storm where a mechanical Zeus rained pretend thunderbolts down on them. Athena made a mental note to tell her dad about that part of the ride after she was back at MOA. She was sure he'd get a kick out of it.

They skirted several islands once the storm had passed. One was full of squealing mechanical pigs that represented sailors the sorceress Circe had turned into swine. (Later the real Odysseus had gotten her to reverse the spell.)

Since there were at least a dozen mechanical gods, monsters, and creatures in the Shipwreck ride, Athena wondered again why Daedalus had only included one—the Minotaur—in the labyrinth. Had he simply run out of time to create more? Either way, the park obviously wasn't a total dud, she was relieved to know. Everyone was going to love this ride for sure. It was scary, adventurous fun!

When the Shipwreck ride was over, the girls went on more rides together, including a sea serpent roller coaster that plunged up and down as if riding the waves on a choppy sea. And another called the Mount Parnassus Special, which involved driving little one-seater golden swans up and down a "mountain" while splashing across flooded "rivers" and being chased by howling mechanical wolves. It was a pretty tame ride, actually.

Athena guessed that it was probably intended for younger riders. Still, she and her friends giggled the whole time, making faces every time they passed each other, and honking at one another to go faster.

At the top of Mount Parnassus in her swan-car, Athena caught a glimpse of Heracles and Theseus across the park grounds. The guys must've finished the bumper chariots, because they were in the game arcade now. She watched Heracles bend a bow and shoot an arrow through a series of axe handles in imitation of a trick Odysseus had done to win back his wife, Penelope, and reclaim his kingdom. Then Athena's swan-car swooped down into a valley, and she lost sight of her crush.

The next time she reached the top of the mountain ride, Heracles and Theseus were gone, probably having moved on to some other game or ride. Medusa and Dionysus were below in the arcade now, though. They were standing near a sign for a game that read: THE PYTHON. There was a giant fanged serpent curled around the two words.

Quickly Athena called to Artemis and pointed the game out. Artemis and Apollo had tangled with the real, riddling Python earlier in the year, and this game seemed to be based on that theme. As the four goddessgirls watched, Dionysus handed Medusa a stuffed toy python he'd apparently just won for her by playing the game.

"How sweet!" cooed Aphrodite.

Then they all screamed with terrified delight as their swan-cars zoomed downhill again.

"Hey! See that sundial?" Persephone called as they came to the end of the ride. "It's noon. Time for the labyrinth to open. Woo-hoo!"

"Let's go!" yelled Artemis. Athena and her friends piled out of their swan-cars. On the way out of the ride, they caught up with a few other students. They all passed back under the grand golden arch, then headed down the columned walkway that led to the red palace door with the gold hinges.

Athena could feel everyone's anticipation and excitement growing as they entered through the door with the bull horns on top and went downstairs to the round brown room. Right away she spotted Heracles and Theseus among a group of students already waiting to enter the labyrinth. A bright blue ribbon that stretched across all three entryways was holding them back, however.

King Minos and Daedalus were standing in front of the ribbon, chatting. Since the king held a large pair of scissors, Athena guessed there was going to be a ribbon-cutting ceremony to mark the opening of the labyrinth.

She would've expected there to be a reporter or two on scene, but come to think of it they were probably all attending the same conference Pheme had gone to in Athens. Had King Minos invited them only to be turned down? How disappointing for him when he wanted to spread the word about his new attraction!

As Athena eyed the archways, her pride in the changes she'd made to the labyrinth swelled. She just hoped Daedalus wouldn't mind that she'd improved it.

Yesterday, before they'd separated and she'd gone off with her friends, he'd told her he was well satisfied that his maze was ready. He'd had other rides to check on, he'd said, and would only return to the labyrinth when it was time to let students enter today.

If the labyrinth became the wild success that she now believed it could be, Daedalus was bound to be happy she'd helped out, right? And she would of course humbly let him take credit for what she'd done.

Ariadne appeared beside her, then wove her way through the group until she managed to insert herself between the two cousins so she could talk to Theseus. Her sparkly pink bag hung over her shoulder. Ye gods. Didn't she go anywhere without it? That girl had been bit by the knitting bug for sure!

Now's my chance to peel Heracles from his cousin's side, thought Athena. But as she moved toward him, Cassandra came up to her. "Hey! I've been meaning to thank you," she began earnestly. "Pheme told me you suggested that she ask Professor Ladon if I could take her place on this trip."

"Apollo was the one who suggested it," Athena said truthfully. "I just seconded him by telling Pheme it was a great idea."

"Oh, but Apollo says Pheme really listens to you," Cassandra told her. "He thinks your support of the idea was crucial."

Athena smiled. "Well, then, I'm glad I could help. Especially since you brought those Opposite Oracle-O cookies on the chariot ride over," she said, grinning. "Dee-lish!"

Cassandra grinned back. But before she could say anything more, King Minos's voice rang out. "This is it, Ladies and Gentlemen. The scary . . . um *very* moment we've all been waiting for."

He must be making the word mix-ups on purpose, Athena decided. They *were* kind of funny, in a weird sort of way.

Minos held his silver scissors up to the blue ribbon. *Snip!* As the ribbon fell away, he called out, "You may now enter the main attraction of Minos's aMAZEment Park—the labyrinth! Have a horrific—I mean, a *terrific* good time," he added, waving them in.

Maybe his way of speaking was some kind of secret code, she thought. A hint that he had a hidden agenda? But, no. Her imagination was just running wild.

The king dramatically swirled his purple cloak over his shoulders and moved away from the three entrances to stand beside Professor Ladon off to one side. "Come on, Professor," he said, rubbing his hands together. "Daedalus can handle things here. And I've been dying to try out those bumper chariots!"

"Bumper chariotsss? Sssounds good to me," the teacher agreed readily. As the two men exited, the king called back over his shoulder to Daedalus, "Keep an eye on things while I'm gone."

Cassandra and Athena fell into line. "I don't know when I've had more fun than today," Cassandra told her. "I just want you to know I really, really appreciate what you did for me. Getting me invited and all."

"Oh, sure. No problem," said Athena, watching help-lessly as Heracles disappeared into the labyrinth up ahead of her with several other students. Theseus wasn't one of them, though. He'd been right behind Heracles when Ariadne had managed to snag him in conversation. And he was still talking to her.

Now that the labyrinth was more complicated, Heracles' head start could make it a lot harder for her to find him inside, Athena feared. She remembered how she'd gotten turned around twice trying to find her way back from the maze's center to the entrance last night. And since she'd left it to her spell to decide on the precise rearrangement of the walls in the other two tunnels, she would have as much trouble as anyone else navigating the newly changed maze. She had absolutely no clue how everything was laid out now.

Smiling brightly, she linked arms with Cassandra and urged her forward. "C'mon. Let's catch up with the others so we can all help each other figure this thing out."

They reached the front of the line at the exact same moment that Theseus broke away from Ariadne to head inside. Only, before he could choose an entrance, Daedalus stepped in front of him. "Sorry," he said. "Just one small group at a time is allowed in. King's orders."

"B-but I was going to hang out with my cousin,"

Theseus sputtered, craning his neck for a glimpse of Heracles beyond the entrance. Daedalus shook his head, holding the boy back. He sent Athena and the others in line an apologetic smile. "You'll all have to wait here and be part of the second group." He must have glimpsed the dismay on her face, because he added quickly, "Fear not. It shouldn't take too long for even the slowest students to make their way in and out."

Theseus let out an annoyed huff. Then he started to pace. Watching him, Athena shifted restlessly from one foot to the other. Given her changes to the maze, she wasn't so sure Daedalus was right. For the first time it occurred to her that he might have made his labyrinth simple on purpose. So that crowds of visitors wouldn't have to wait too long for a turn inside it. Uh-oh. She couldn't quite bring herself to tell Daedalus what she'd done, however. And she lost her chance to try when a messenger sent by the king came up to him a minute later.

"Slight problem with one of the bumper chariots," she overheard the messenger murmur into his ear. Athena caught the words "flames" and "smash-up." Had Professor Ladon gotten a little too excited playing bumper chariots and accidentally set his chariot on fire during an especially violent collision?

The messenger didn't seem agitated, so it seemed likely there was no real reason for alarm. After urging the remaining students to wait their turn until the first group had completed the maze, Daedalus put them on their honor and hurried off with the messenger.

As the minutes ticked by, Athena distracted herself from her concern about how the students inside the labyrinth were faring by chitchatting with her friends. However, when not one of the group who'd gone in first had reappeared in the next half hour, she started to panic in earnest. In her zeal to make the labyrinth more challenging, it seemed possible she'd succeeded far *too* well.

"I wonder what's taking so long," said Cassandra.

"Good question," said Apollo. "I can understand why Artemis isn't out yet, though. She has no sense of direction. She wouldn't even be able to find her way out of a papyrus bag!"

Cassandra giggled. It was true, thought Athena. But Cassandra wouldn't be laughing if she knew Athena had made the maze mega-hard. Too hard for someone with no sense of direction. Something Athena hadn't thought about when she'd altered the maze. She hoped Artemis wasn't lost and alone in there.

"But Artemis aside, where's everyone else?" Apollo continued. He was starting to look worried too.

Athena took note of who was still waiting outside

the labyrinth with her—Persephone, Pandora, Theseus, Apollo, Cassandra, Ariadne, and Medusa. Which meant that Heracles, Artemis, Aphrodite, Ares, Hades, and Dionysus were still inside. Also Actaeon. So maybe Artemis was with him. She hoped so.

After fifteen more minutes went by, everyone grew restless and worried. Theseus was still pacing to and fro in front of the entrances, stopping every now and then to peer inside. Ariadne had taken her knitting from her sparkly pink bag. Her needles clicked together nervously as she added another row of stitches to the scarf she was making. It was a scarf that Ms. Hydra, Zeus's nine-headed administrative assistant back at MOA, would've loved, Athena thought. Because it was long enough to wrap around all nine of her necks!

Persephone had been chatting with Medusa, but now she came over to Athena. "You've been inside the labyrinth," she said. "Any idea why it could be taking Hades and the others so long to find their way out?"

Athena wrinkled her brow. "I . . . um . . ."

Persephone drew her aside. "What's wrong?" she asked. "I can tell you're worried about something. Come on. Spill."

After several more moments of hesitation, Athena began to confess what she'd done and why. As she described the spells she'd cast to disconnect and move apart the walls, Persephone turned even paler than usual.

"Parts of the Underworld are labyrinth-like," she told Athena in a low voice. "And Hades once told me that the areas with 'complex' mazes are nearly impossible to get out of. Even *he* has trouble and gets lost in them sometimes. And he knows every inch of them since he's been in them dozens of times!"

"Really?" Athena felt all color drain from her face. She

probably looked as pale as Persephone right now! "What do you think I should do, then?" she whispered plaintively. But before Persephone could reply, Hades wandered out of the maze. He was limping.

Relieved to see him, Persephone and Athena rushed to his side. "Am I the first person out?" he asked, looking around in surprise. Both goddessgirls nodded in reply as all the other waiting students gathered around him.

Hades slumped against the wall. "Gotta get off my ankle," he said. He slid down till he was sitting on the floor.

Persephone dropped to crouch beside him. "What happened? How did you hurt it?" she asked anxiously.

"Twisted it tripping over a stalagmite," Hades explained. Then, speaking in a grave voice, he told everyone, "That maze is way too hard. I don't know what Daedalus could have been thinking designing it that way. I only found my way out by pure dumb luck. The rest of the group must still be wandering around in there."

Athena opened her mouth, planning to admit to Hades and the others what she'd already told Persephone in private. Before she could say a word, however, an ear-splitting series of roars erupted from somewhere deep within the labyrinth. These were closely followed by terrified screams. The MOA students, Theseus, Cassandra, and Ariadne stared at one another in shock.

8

Ariadne's Scarf

*G*RRR! GRRR!

"Was that the . . . the Minotaur?" Persephone asked, her green eyes wide.

"It was switched off when Daedalus showed it to me," said Athena. "But those roars sounded just like the Minotaurs in the Forest of the Beasts, so maybe . . ."

"We used to hear roars like that while Daedalus was building the labyrinth," Ariadne interrupted. "Dad wouldn't allow me near the monster *or* the labyrinth, though. I always thought he was, like, soo overprotective. Now I'm kind of thinking he was right."

Hades winced as he stretched his hurt ankle out in front of him. "The truth is, I never made it to the center of the maze, so I don't know if the Minotaur is switched on or off. I was maybe halfway in there before I got totally lost. Like I said, I was lucky to find my way out again."

Several more deep and ferocious roars split the air, followed by more screams.

"Do you think those could be the happy screams of kids having fun?" Pandora asked hopefully. When everyone gave her an *Are you crazy?* look, she sighed. "Well, nothing wrong with asking."

"The Minotaur's mechanical, right? It couldn't really harm anyone, could it?" asked Medusa. There was an edge of worry to her voice too. And no wonder. Medusa's crush, Dionysus, was among those inside the labyrinth. Athena knew how she felt. Not only was Heracles in the maze. Her BFFs Aphrodite and Artemis were in there too!

"We have to do something. Fight back somehow," said Apollo. He looked ready to race inside the maze.

"Apollo's right. We should attack," agreed Theseus. "Heracles may have battled and defeated tons of monsters," he added, "but he doesn't have his trusty club with him this time. And his strength alone might not be enough to fend off a Minotaur gone haywire."

Athena's jaw tensed as she remembered how dangerous the magical beasts in the Forest of the Beasts had become when *they* had gone haywire once. "We definitely need to get everyone out of there, and the sooner the better, but—"

"I'll go after them!" exclaimed Theseus. He'd been kneeling beside Hades, but now he leaped to his feet and dashed toward the center archway.

"Wait. Stop!" Athena called after him. He drew up short and spun around to look at her.

"You said 'the sooner the better,'" he said with a frown. "My cousin needs me, and we're all just standing around talking!"

"He's right," Medusa said. "So while you're all deciding what to do here, I'll go find Professor Ladon, King Minos, and that wacky inventor who dreamed up this crazy maze. He probably knows the way in."

"Good idea. I'll go with you to the bumper chariots," Apollo volunteered. The two of them took off just as the monster let out another mighty *ROAARRR*.

Athena shuddered. Earlier she'd been wishing that Daedalus had put even more mechanical monsters inside the labyrinth. Now she was very glad he hadn't. Because maybe even one was too many!

"I'm going in there," Theseus said stubbornly.

Athena suspected that the boy's eagerness to be off was due to more than just concern for Heracles. He wanted to prove himself a hero, a desire that was probably every bit as important to him as inventing things was to her. And what better way to prove his heroism than by rescuing the cousin whose courage he so much admired and respected?

"No way," squeaked Ariadne. "You'll only wind up hurt or trapped like those who are in there now."

Glancing across the room, Persephone caught Athena's gaze and said to her, "Don't you think there's something you should tell every—"

With the smallest of movements Athena shook her head. She knew Persephone wanted her to fess up about what she'd done. But right now the important thing was getting everyone out. The news about who'd made the maze more difficult wouldn't help matters, and she didn't want to waste time playing the blame game.

And there was another important reason for keeping mum, that her friend didn't know.

Athena didn't want to draw attention to the problem she'd seen in Daedalus's design—that the maze had been too easy. That could ruin his chances for the fame and glory he truly deserved for having thought it up in the first place.

However, her third reason for keeping quiet was not so noble. Her pride. She didn't want everyone to know what a huge mistake she'd made!

Abruptly the monster roared again, making both girls jump. It was louder than ever. So were the students' screams that followed. They were making Athena so jittery that her usual dependably bright brain wasn't cooperating. *Think, think, think!* she told herself. She had to formulate a plan to fix things—fast.

"Maybe you could see what's happening?" Pandora suggested anxiously to Cassandra. "Or see the path we should take?"

With a confused expression on her face, Ariadne looked from one girl to the other.

"Cassandra can prophesy," Persephone quickly explained.

Cassandra closed her eyes, and everyone fell quiet so she could concentrate. While she was doing that, Persephone jumped up and beckoned to Athena to follow her. When they were far enough away from the others that they couldn't easily be overheard, Perse-phone whispered, "You really don't remember well enough all the changes you made to the maze? You couldn't find your way in and out of it again?"

Athena shook her head. "No. I wish I could. And un-spelling the walls to return them to their original positions would be risky. The moving walls might accidentally crush the students inside. Or make the Minotaur even madder."

Persephone opened her mouth again, and Athena feared her friend was about to scold her for her part in this. But just then Cassandra's eyes popped open. "I'm so sorry," she said. "I couldn't see anything."

"Probably too dark in there," Ariadne said.

Athena and Persephone turned to stare at her. Did she really not understand the difference between seeing into the future and actual seeing? Athena wondered. From the look on Persephone's face, she was doubtless wondering the same thing. If Ariadne had ever been inside the labyrinth, she would have known that there were torches to light the passageways. Did she think that her dad and Daedalus would let visitors wander around in the dark? As nice as Ariadne was, she honestly did seem to be a bit of an airhead.

Not seeming to notice their reactions, Ariadne pulled her pink scarf-in-progress from her bag again. But instead of starting to work on her project, she only stared down at it. With a furrowed brow she slipped the scarf off her needles, which she stuck back into her bag. Using two fingers she pulled on the loose end of the string of yarn, and watched the scarf slowly unravel. Maybe, Athena thought, she'd finally realized that the thing had gotten much too long.

"I'll go with Theseus," Hades said suddenly. He struggled to stand, but then moaned and quickly sank back down.

Persephone ran back over to him, shaking her head.

"No way, Mr. Underworld. You're not going anywhere with that bum ankle."

"I'll go by myself," Theseus insisted. With renewed determination he took a step into the center tunnel.

ROAAAR! ROAAAR! ROAAAR! The Minotaur's bellows echoed down the passageways.

"AAAAAAHH!" screamed the students inside.

Theseus halted. He glanced over his shoulder at Athena. It was almost as if he were hoping she'd try to stop him again, she thought. Was it possible he wasn't quite as courageous as he pretended to be? Or maybe he just wanted her to go in with him!

"Okay. If you're going, I'll go with you," she said. Though the chance was high that they'd only get lost, she was out of other ideas.

"Oh. My. Godz!" Ariadne exclaimed suddenly.

As everyone turned to look at her, she held up

her too-long pink scarf. "I just got the best idea!" she announced. Smiling, she scurried over to Theseus. "Take this with you," she said, handing him the scarf.

"A *pink* scarf? That's your idea? You want me to put your scarf around my neck so I'll stay warm—not to mention *girly*-looking—in the labyrinth?" he asked in appalled confusion.

"No, silly," said Ariadne. "Tie it around your waist. I'll stay out here and hold on to the loose end of the yarn. The scarf will unravel with each step you take away from me, more and more the farther you go into the maze. And that way you won't get lost because you can always follow the yarn trail back out."

Athena stared at the girl in surprise. "That's a brilliant idea!" she exclaimed. The others nodded enthusiastically.

"I should have foreseen it," Cassandra murmured.

I should have come up with it myself, thought Athena. Ariadne was obviously cleverer than Athena had originally assumed.

Theseus tied the scarf around his waist, then grinned at the princess as he handed her back the loose end of the pink yarn to hold. "Wish me luck," he said, glancing around at the group.

"We do!" they all replied at the same time.

Athena started to go with him, but he held out a hand to stop her. "No need," he said, dismissing her help. As he plunged into the tunnel, the scarf began to unravel in a long pink line behind him. For a long moment everyone stared after him, silent.

Then Persephone turned to Ariadne. "I feel kind of bad about your scarf."

"Yeah," said Athena. "You spent so much time working on it."

Ariadne shrugged like it was no big deal. "It was okay for a first effort," she said, glancing up at them through long dark lashes. "But I'll need, like, a *lot* more practice before I can control those needles enough to actually knit something worth keeping."

Control? All at once Athena remembered something she'd forgotten until now. Something important that Daedalus had told her. There was a *control* room somewhere in the palace. She'd probably made a big mistake changing the labyrinth, but if she could find the room that controlled the Minotaur, maybe she could still assist in putting things right. Meanwhile, with the help of Ariadne's plan, Theseus had at least a chance of rescuing those caught in the maze.

Pulling Persephone aside, Athena explained what she hoped to accomplish. Then, leaving her friends, she raced upstairs.

Behind her the Minotaur's roars sounded again. Like thunder after lightning, screams immediately followed from deep within the labyrinth, sending chills up her spine.

9

Sparks Fly

ATHENA BURST OUT THROUGH THE RED DOOR.
She glanced down the walkway, toward the entrance to
the rides and games area of the aMAZEment Park. She
was hoping to see Daedalus, King Minos, and Professor Ladon coming toward her, accompanied by Medusa
and Apollo. But no such luck. Since the bumper chariot
ride was at the far end of the park, it would probably
take Medusa and Apollo a while to get there. And even

more time for all of them to make it back to the laby-rinth.

Well, she couldn't wait that long for Daedalus to save the day. Even out here Athena could still hear the roars and screams coming from down in the maze. She dashed around the palace till she reached the main palace doors. There was no time to lose!

After passing through the banquet hall, she began to weave her way through a series of passageways that opened off into lots of small chambers within the palace. Though she'd never been in the control room, she knew it was located above the Minotaur in the maze, which meant that the room had to be somewhere near the center of the palace.

Athena turned down another passageway. The palace was huge! Luckily, she had a better sense of direction than her friend Artemis. Apollo hadn't been exaggerating *too* much when he'd said that his sister couldn't find her way out of a papyrus bag!

As she ran, the monstrous roars of the Minotaur got even louder, reverberating up through the mosaic-tiled floor beneath her feet. She must be getting closer!

She'd been opening doors as she went along. Most of the rooms in this wing of the palace were storerooms that housed large clay containers called pithoi. She didn't need to peek inside the pithoi to know that they held foods such as oil, grains, dried fish, beans, and, of course, *olives*, the fruit of her best-known, best-loved invention.

Athena passed servants now and then, but when she tried to question a group of them, she realized they spoke a dialect of Greek that she didn't understand. She tried acting out what she was looking for, making gestures to pretend she was moving imaginary controls. Then she held up one finger on each side of her head as if they were horns, stamping her feet and snorting, hoping they'd get the idea that she was looking for the room where Daedalus controlled the Minotaur. But when the servants only laughed at her antics, she gave up on them and continued searching for the control room on her own.

The Minotaur's roars had grown deafening now. But the screams that had followed them had stopped. What did it mean? Had Theseus rescued them already? Or had something dire happened to her friends instead? Had they been munched, mangled, or Minotaured into oblivion? *Gulp!*

Trying not to think the worst, Athena threw open yet another door . . . and stepped into a room that hummed with machinery. *Yes!* This had to be Daedalus's workshop. And that meant she was directly over the center of the labyrinth!

She made her way past a workbench crowded with nuts, bolts, tools, and pieces of metal and wood. Soon she was standing before a desk-size machine of shifting gears, switches, knobs, buttons, handles, pulleys, and levers in the very center of the room. This must be the control board!

Hearing a noise, she glanced across the room toward a door. She saw a flash of gold, and then it was gone. Had that door just opened and closed? she wondered. But she had no time to investigate.

Right away she saw that the floor beneath the control board was made of thick, clear glass. Dropping to her hands and knees, she peered down through it. About twenty feet below her the Minotaur bellowed and raged alone in its room. It stamped its hooves and snorted, and thrust its head with its wickedly sharp horns this way and that.

Athena gasped when in the very next moment, down below, Theseus rushed in to confront the ferocious mechanical beast. Although the pink yarn stretched out behind him, he wasn't wearing the scarf anymore. It must have gotten too short to tie around his waist. What was left of it he seemed to have stuffed into the pocket of his tunic.

But where were Heracles and the other students? she wondered. They wouldn't have sent Theseus there on his own if they'd met up with him in the maze. Especially the guys, who all loved a good fight. Had the trapped students already been searching for a way out before Theseus arrived? Had they found his yarn trail on their own? Were they now following it back out of the labyrinth? She hoped so!

Athena banged on the glass floor, trying to let Theseus know that she was above him in the control room, but he didn't seem to hear. She remembered Daedalus saying that this glass was one-way. So although she could see Theseus, he wouldn't be able to see her even if he did hear the banging and look up. When he yelled something a few seconds later, she couldn't hear him, either. The Minotaur roared again. *That* she could hear. The monster was incredibly loud! Lowering its head, the beast lunged toward Theseus.

If the others had already found their way out, why had he continued to the maze's center instead of following the yarn back to safety too? she wondered. Was it possible he was trying to keep the monster at bay while they made their escape? That would be pretty brave of him, actually. Daedalus had told her that the mechanical monster couldn't take more than a few steps in any one direction, but Theseus didn't know that. For all he knew, the monster really might charge him at any moment. And then go after his friends. And thrash them all to smithereens!

Just then something silver flashed in Theseus's hand. *Ye gods.* Athena groaned aloud when she realized what it was. His daggerlike sword. It must have been hidden under his tunic! She'd known since the ride to Crete that he'd brought it with him, of course. Still, after Heracles had scolded him for trying to show it off in the banquet hall and warned him that he could get in trouble for bringing it, she'd figured Theseus would have had the good sense to leave it in his room. Apparently not.

Clang! Theseus struck out at the monster with his puny sword. Athena gasped. Horrified, she saw that the foolish boy really did intend to *fight* the Minotaur. Alone. With a weapon that was so short, he had to move in dangerously close to the beast to strike it. As metal connected with metal, sparks flew.

ROAAAR! bellowed the Minotaur. Big puffs of smoke blasted from its nostrils. Its eyes glowed red and fierce. Theseus took a step back as the monster lowered its head and lunged at him. *Clang!* Theseus struck again.

Jolted into action, Athena leaped to her feet. Frantically she studied the machine that stood in the middle of the floor, which she knew must control the Minotaur. But which lever, knob, or other doohickey on this control panel was the on-off switch?

Clang! Clang! ROAAAR! Choosing a lever at random, Athena slid it from left to right. *ROAAAR!* She winced, her hands automatically flying to cover her ears. Oops! She'd accidentally chosen the switch that controlled the volume of the monster's bellows. When she slid it left again, the roars died away till she could barely hear them. *Phew!* That was a relief to her ears.

Choosing another lever, Athena yanked it upward. Instantly the snorts of smoke quit shooting from the Minotaur's nostrils. She tried other levers, knobs, buttons, and handles, one after the other. One lever made the beast's tail swish. Yet another made its fierce red eyes start spinning around like a windmill.

Down below, Theseus and the Minotaur battled on. She had to get that crazy boy and his weapon out of there! She didn't want him to get hurt, for sure. But she also didn't want him to harm the Minotaur. It was the labyrinth's star attraction, and if it was destroyed, Daedalus's maze would be ruined.

Clang! Clang! Roar.

The Minotaur turned in a circle. *Godsamighty.* Wrong lever again!

Then out of the corner of her eye Athena saw a button she hadn't noticed before. A small one that was painted red. *Hmm.* None of the other controls were painted a color. So there had to be something special about that one, right? And what could be more special than an on-off switch?

Clang! ROAR. Clang! Clang! Clang! Theseus's attack on the Minotaur was growing more and more frenzied.

"Fingers crossed," Athena whispered to herself.

Hoping that she'd guessed right about the red button, she reached out . . . and pushed it.

And just like that, the Minotaur went still. No more roars, no more smoke-snorts, no more spinning fiery red eyes. No movement at all. Thank godness!

"Yes! Take that, you monster!" Now that the Minotaur was turned off and no longer making noise she could hear Theseus's victorious shout even from twenty feet above. He was wildly, loudly excited. She watched through the glass floor as he thrust his sword high. "Woo-hoo! I did it!" He did a silly little victory dance, hopping from one foot to the other, then took a victory lap around the room. He was convinced he'd defeated the monster all by himself!

"Athena?"

She'd been concentrating so hard that she jumped in surprise when Daedalus practically popped out of nowhere and spoke her name. "Oh! You scared me," she told him.

He frowned at her, seeming a little annoyed to find her here. "How did you—" He stopped short, his eyes roving the controls. Then he glanced down through the glass floor, and his face relaxed. "You found the on-off button. Well, thank goodness for that. Medusa and Apollo told me there was trouble in the labyrinth, but I don't know how it—"

"I do," Athena interrupted him. "And it's all my fault."

"Huh?" Daedalus's brow wrinkled in confusion. "I don't really see how that could be possible."

She looked down through the glass floor and saw that the Minotaur was alone again. Theseus was gone. With an inward sigh, she headed for the door. "C'mon. We'd better get back to the labyrinth entrance and see what's up. Theseus is okay, but I want to check on the others." She knew she had to explain things and tell Daedalus what she had done, but she sure wasn't looking forward to it.

As she started out of the room, Daedalus said, "Wait. There's a quicker way to get to the maze's center." He led her to the small door in the corner of the workshop where she'd seen the flash of gold earlier.

When he opened the door, Athena peered into a winding chute that went downward. Uh-oh. In spite of what he'd said before, had he actually figured out that she'd changed the maze? Was he planning to push her down this chute to some palace dungeon as punishment? Even though the idea was ridiculous—no mortal would *dare* punish an immortal, no matter what mischief they'd made—she took a cautious step backward.

"It's for emergencies," he explained. "We can slide down it, and it'll put us at the center of the labyrinth near the Minotaur room. If there are any students left inside, we can help them find the way out."

"Okay," Athena agreed in relief. "That sounds pretty cool, actually. You first, though," she said, just in case.

After they'd both whooshed down the chute, they exited through a door in the wall. Daedalus looked around. "That's odd," he said. "The walls here seem closer together than I remember." Then he noticed a free-standing section of wall almost directly in front of them.

He frowned, and his eyebrows knit together. "Where did that come from?"

Athena gulped. She wouldn't blame him if, when she explained what she'd done, he lost all the respect and admiration he'd once had for her. *Arghh!*

10
Humble Pie

LAST NIGHT AFTER DINNER I DISCONNECTED some of the walls and moved them around," Athena confessed in a rush as they stood deep inside the maze.

Daedalus turned to stare at her, a look of astonishment on his face. "What? But why?"

Her cheeks burned with embarrassment. "Um, I wanted to make the labyrinth more difficult. I thought it might add to the, uh, fun."

She followed Daedalus as he circled the out-of-place wall. "So you thought it was too easy?" he asked.

"Maybe a little," Athena fudged, circling it behind him. "But I think my changes made the maze *too* hard. That's why my friends got trapped." She took a deep breath as they entered the blood-red hexagonal room at the center of the maze. As hard as it was to admit everything, she knew it was the right thing to do. "So you see, all that's gone wrong here really is my fault, and I'm truly sorry for the trouble I've caused."

Spying the Minotaur, which was frozen in place with its head thrown back midroar, Daedalus hurried over to it and began checking it for damage. He patted his mechanical beast on the back in concern, frowning at the dents that Theseus's sword had made on its arms and legs. "For Zeus's sake! What happened to you, fella?"

Athena opened her mouth to explain about Theseus's fight with the Minotaur, but then she closed it again. Daedalus might get mad at him, which wouldn't be fair. And if Daedalus told Professor Ladon and the king, they'd blame Theseus too. Even if Theseus had fought the monster with the best of intentions, he'd get in trouble for bringing his sword on the trip. No. This whole disaster was *her* responsibility.

"Well, when the Minotaur wouldn't stop roaring, I think some of the students might've gotten scared and lashed out at it," she explained. "It kind of went berserk, puffing smoke from its nostrils and lashing out with its claws. And roaring." She shuddered. "Scary."

"It has a voice sensor that's triggered whenever visitors come within a few feet of it. If even one person goes near it, it'll keep on bellowing," said Daedalus as he continued examining his Minotaur. "So it's meant to be frightening, yes. But it's actually pretty harmless. Still, I don't understand why it went so out of control. I didn't set the levers to do all those things—the continuous roars and the smoke and all that."

Athena shrugged. It was nice that he was taking all this so calmly. "I can fix those dents in your Minotaur," she offered. "And I can un-spell the walls and return them to their original positions too. But first let's make sure everyone else is out of the maze. Wouldn't want to crush anyone."

"They're out," said Daedalus, perking up at her offer. "I saw them all in the room where you enter the labyrinth before I came up here, and Theseus must have found his way back out by now too. So, go ahead. I've always wanted to see real magic performed."

Athena grinned, then waved a hand toward the Minotaur and chanted:

"*Dents undo.*

Be as good as new."

Pop! Pop! Pop! The Minotaur's dents began magically pushing themselves out, until not a trace of its injuries remained.

"Amazing!" Daedalus said, laughing in delight. "I should put you to work on the bumper chariots. Professor Ladon and King Minos went a little crazy on that ride, like two big kids."

"I'd be happy to fix—" she started to offer, but he shook his head, anticipating what she was going to say.

"No worries. I've already got some guys working on them," he told her. "The ride'll be as good as new by tomorrow when we reopen the park for mortals and everyone else to visit."

"Okay. Now the walls," said Athena, glancing around.

"Let's start moving toward the exit, and I'll change things behind us as we go." As they began walking, she did a chant to un-spell the walls:

"Let former moving spells erase,
So all these walls shift back in place."

Crack! Rumble. Snap! As the two inventors walked through the maze, the walls behind them moved, splitting or merging until they returned to their original positions. It was like the spell was following them and fixing things up.

"Wait. I have an idea," said Daedalus. When they paused, the walls behind them stopped moving too. "You made the labyrinth more complicated for a reason, right? Because it was boring."

"Oh—well," she started to protest. "I didn't say that exactly."

"It's okay. I can take it," said Daedalus. "We inventors have to be open to suggestions. And I was a little worried about the level of difficulty myself. So I vote that we leave some of the changes you made but put some walls back the way I originally had them."

Athena's eyes brightened with delight. "So that your maze is more complicated but not *too* complicated? Yeah! I love it!" She paused, thinking. "Maybe the most complicated part should be near the center? And the outer walls closer to the entrance could go back to the simpler way you had them?"

"Perfect," said Daedalus. They discussed the wall changes as they went, and Athena cast more spells so that the maze became a real blend of their ideas, with some easy pathways and some more difficult ones.

Noticing a red-and-blue-striped stalactite above his head, Daedalus pointed up at it. "An addition of yours?"

"Um, yeah," she said. "I also added a few gargoyles. Want me to take them out?" She raised a hand toward them, ready to say a "remove" chant.

"No!" he said. "I like them."

Athena grinned and lowered her arm. "Okay. They stay."

"Thanks," he said. He was turning in a circle now, gazing happily at the new, improved maze. "This is so much better than how I had it."

"Better than how I had it too, right?" Athena said, laughing.

He laughed with her. "Everyone who visits is going to go crazy over it. Let's hear it for mortal-immortal team-work."

"High five," said Athena, and they slapped hands. Then she added, "After messing things up, putting them right again was the least I could do."

"Don't beat yourself up about this," Daedalus urged as they walked on. "Nobody got hurt really. Besides, I've made worse mistakes." His eyes twinkled as he added, "It's actually kind of a relief to know that the goddess I admire above all others can occasionally make a mistake too."

"More than occasionally," Athena corrected him. "When I first got to MOA, I invented a shampoo that accidentally turned Medusa's hair to snakes. And that's only *one* example." Daedalus grinned.

She couldn't believe that the most famous mortal inventor and architect on Earth had called her "the goddess I admire above all others." How cool was that! Still, as pleasing as the praise was, she hoped he now saw that she was just as imperfect as anyone else. Because perfection was pretty much an impossible standard to live up to.

"So what's been your worst mistake ever?" she asked him curiously as they neared the exit.

Daedalus laughed. "That's easy. A dance floor I designed for Princess Ariadne. The floor was beautiful, if I do say so myself. Problem was, I put a thick layer of wax on top of it and polished it to make it shine." He shot her a sheepish glance. "Which made the floor so slippery that the dancers who tried it out the very first time slipped and slid into each other."

Athena couldn't help giggling, imagining what a crazy scene that must have been. "It *was* pretty funny!" he said, joining in her laughter. "They wound up with bumps and bruises galore, but luckily no broken bones." He shook his head at the memory. "If I'd simply done a small test of that wax on the floor and tried it out right away, I would've realized my mistake and been able to avoid the *slippery* problem."

She thought about that. What if she'd suggested her maze wall changes to Daedalus the *first* time he'd shown her the labyrinth? If only she'd guessed he'd be strong enough to take constructive criticism. They could've tried the changes out before the grand opening and avoided the mistakes she'd made in changing everything on her own.

When they reached the room at the entrance to the labyrinth, they found King Minos and Professor Ladon. Athena was relieved to see all the other students there too, appearing unhurt. Those who'd been caught in the maze were eagerly describing their adventure while the other students and the two men sat on the stairs to listen.

"The Minotaur kept lunging at us," Actaeon was saying, imitating the movements of the beast as Athena and Daedalus quietly stood at the back of the group.

"Yeah, that thing can *roar*. It was terrifying," said Artemis. "I've never been so scared—or lost—in my life!"

Athena and Daedalus looked at each other, worry in their eyes. Would the king decide the Minotaur maze was too scary and close down the labyrinth forever? Maybe even close the whole park?

No one had noticed the two of them yet. Athena leaned over and whispered to Daedalus. "Was King Minos mad about that dance floor fiasco?"

Daedalus shook his head. "Believe it or not, he laughed like you did."

"That's good. Let's just hope he finds this labyrinth incident as hilarious," she whispered back. She held up her crossed fingers to show him, and he did the same back. The two of them lingered near the arched entrances to the maze, listening in as the students went on describing their time inside the labyrinth.

"It was wild. Freaky," said Heracles.

"Out of control!" Ares crowed.

"Wicked," added Actaeon.

"It was sooo . . . fun!" Aphrodite finished, a smile breaking across her pretty face. "It was mega-tastic!"

"Yeah," said Artemis. "The best!"

Dionysus's violet eyes lit up. "And every time we tried to find our way out we wound up right back in the middle with the monster!" He laughed, remembering.

Daedalus and Athena looked at each other again, this time in total surprise.

"So you liked it?" Persephone asked the group of students who'd just come out of the maze. They all nodded.

"I guess I would have too," Hades told her. "If I hadn't tripped. That was kind of embarrassing, not to mention painful."

"But the maze *was* sort of hard," Artemis admitted. "So we weren't too sorry when we spied Theseus's pink

185

yarn trail and were able to find our way back out."

At that, Athena's gaze found Theseus, who was sitting toward the middle of the stairs near Ariadne, helping her rewind a mountain of tangled pink yarn into several large balls. This was, of course, the yarn that had followed him out of the labyrinth as he'd threaded his way back after "vanquishing" the Minotaur.

Daedalus finally spoke up, drawing everyone's attention. "Last night Athena and I decided the maze was too easy, so we made it harder. Maybe too hard. But we've changed things again, so I think the next group in will find it a little easier now."

"But not too easy, I hope," the king said quickly, which surprised Athena. Had he guessed the original maze was too uncomplicated?

Daedalus grinned, shaking his head. "No worries."

He wasn't just a great inventor, Athena decided. He

was also *kind*. He'd taken half the blame for the maze being too hard, when it had been entirely her fault. The two of them stepped forward to the center of the room.

Professor Ladon shot the group of students who'd been in the maze a puzzled look. "I don't underssstand. Why were you ssscreaming if you liked the experience ssso much?" The ones nearest him fanned their noses when he looked away. He really could use some mega-breath mints!

"Because sometimes being scared is fun!" Aphrodite explained. "Especially when you know you're actually safe."

King Minos was beaming. "So it was *really* fun, then? Great!"

"We had a little ssscare of our own," the professor mused. "A big crash with flamesss and the like. But it wasss fun, too, sssince we knew we were ssstill sssafe in thossse padded bumper chariotsss." He glanced at the king. "By the way, where did you get off to there at the end? When Medusssa and Apollo arrived we couldn't find you."

Before Minos could reply, Medusa piped up. "So do the rest of us get to go through the labyrinth or what?" she asked in an impatient tone.

At her question King Minos leaped to his sandaled feet. He looked a little relieved at not having to answer the professor, Athena noticed. "Of course. Just be careful and stay calm," he called out in a mock stern voice. Then he smiled at the students. "As some of you have already had the pleasure to learn firsthand, the star attraction of Minos's aMAZEment Park is a chilling . . . I mean a *thrilling* experience!"

After swirling his purple cloak over his shoulders, he strode up to the arched opening into the labyrinth. "Well, come on," he called to the eager students who had yet to go inside. With a teasing look at Professor Ladon, he said, "Last one in is a rotten dinosaur egg."

As he dashed off, his crown caught the light from a torch. When a flash of gold blinded Athena for a second, she frowned. That momentary flash had reminded her of something.

"That won't be me!" shouted Professor Ladon as he jumped up and rushed through the arched opening behind the king. Medusa, Pandora, Apollo, and the other students who hadn't yet had a turn inside the labyrinth raced after him.

"That's it!" Athena said suddenly. As she, Daedalus, and the students who'd already toured the maze headed upstairs and outside, she spoke to him in a low voice. "Remember what my teacher said about King Minos disappearing after the bumper chariot crash? I think it was the king who messed up those controls!"

She explained about seeing the flash of gold as she'd entered the control room and how it had looked like the flash of his crown just now. "He must have come back here before Medusa, Apollo, and Professor Ladon. He must have sneaked upstairs before me and then run off again when I arrived."

"But why would he do that?" asked the inventor.

"No clue," she replied. "Maybe, like me, he was trying to turn the Minotaur off?"

"Maybe," Daedalus said uncertainly. Then his brows rose. "Or maybe he was up there trying to make it even scarier. He sure seemed happy that everyone had such a screaming good time."

Athena grinned. "Ha! I bet you're right. In fact, that's probably what all his weird little word mix-ups were about. You must have heard them too. He wanted the

Minotaur in the maze to be both 'chilling' and 'thrilling,' for instance."

"Yeah!" said Daedalus. "And he wanted everyone to have a 'frightful, delightful' experience too."

Nodding, Athena glanced over at Theseus. He and Ariadne hadn't gone into the labyrinth with the second group. And they weren't heading off into the park to the other rides now like students from the first group. Instead the pair were chatting away about his adventure on a bench outside as they continued to wind the pink yarn into balls. There was no harm in Theseus believing that he'd actually slain the monster, Athena decided. He'd *thought* there was danger and had acted bravely in the face of it. He deserved his moment of glory!

All at once Daedalus froze. "Yikes. Later!" he said to Athena. "Just remembered I need to turn the Minotaur back on before that second group finds its way to the middle of the maze." He took a few steps, then looked back at her. "Want to come? I could explain the whole control center to you."

Out of the corner of her eye Athena noticed that Heracles was coming over. He was staring at her and Daedalus, and there was a scowl on his face. Was it possible he was a little jealous? Of Daedalus? He had no reason to be, of course. Besides, it was his own fault that she'd been spending more time with Daedalus than with him. But then she softened. Probably Heracles just missed her like she missed *him*. As he drew nearer, she quickly told Daedalus she'd meet him in the control room in just a few minutes.

"What's up?" Heracles asked her. By the time he reached her side, his scowl had disappeared. "I can sense there's more to the story of what happened in the maze than Daedalus told everyone."

"Yeah. There's some stuff I should tell you," said Athena.

As they walked a little ways into the park together, she explained everything. That Daedalus had only been being kind when he'd implied that he'd been partly responsible for the labyrinth's complexity. And that it had been she alone who'd gone downstairs during dinner the night before to make changes.

Hearing this, Heracles looked shocked, but a little pleased, too. Was it just her imagination, or did he seem relieved that Daedalus and she were just friends with a mutual interest in inventing? If so, that had to mean Heracles wasn't planning to dump her like had happened to that seven-headed Hydra-lady she'd read about in the Supernatural Market scrollazine. He must still want to be her crush, right?

Since Heracles already knew that Theseus had brought

his short sword on the trip, Athena recounted his cousin's "battle" with the Minotaur. She thought that Heracles, at least, should know about the boy's attempted heroism.

Heracles' expression filled with pride as he looked over his shoulder. She followed his gaze to where Theseus and Ariadne were now walking side by side in the park. They were laughing, chatting, and still winding yarn together.

"That yarn idea of Ariadne's was brilliant," she mused aloud. She had truly misjudged the girl. Just as she'd misjudged Daedalus, thinking she knew better than he did what the design of the labyrinth should be. Suddenly she felt quite humble.

Heracles nodded, and they continued on their own walk, discussing the rides they passed and the ones they'd been on. "Did you try the Twelve Labors ride?"

She shook her head. "I didn't get the chance."

"The Hydra labor part is cool—you get to ride on the moving heads. And the Erymanthian boar section was wicked epic. You'd like it," Heracles told her. He'd begun to sound a little distracted. Something had caught his eye. She looked over to see that Theseus was alone now. Ariadne was heading back toward the palace with a servant.

"Yeah, you should try that ride," Heracles said to Athena. "Well, see you." With that, he started toward his cousin.

Huh? He wasn't asking her to go *with* him on the ride?

Just then she remembered how Heracles had told Theseus that his favorite labors had been two of the ones he'd done *without* her help. "Are you sure you didn't prefer the Geryon part of the ride? Or maybe the man-eating horses section?" she called after him.

He stopped and turned to look at her with an expression that was confused and a bit wary. "Are you mad about something?"

Annoyed and hurt, she said coolly, "You figure it out. I've got to go. Daedalus is going to explain the control room to me while the second group does the maze." Without another word she took off for the palace and raced inside.

Daedalus was in the control room by the time she arrived. He'd already turned on the Minotaur, but now he explained to her how everything worked. It was so fascinating that she stopped thinking about Heracles as she listened. Mostly stopped, anyway.

As the two of them watched through the glass floor, waiting for the students to appear in the Minotaur room below, Athena found herself asking his advice about how to improve the plow she'd invented.

Daedalus listened intently as she described how it

worked. Then he asked, "What do you most want your improvements to do?"

"Make it take less effort to use," Athena answered readily. "You see, farmers tell me that the plow works great, but pushing it is hard, sweaty work."

"Hmm," said Daedalus, rubbing his chin in thought. "A sharper blade and more comfortable handles might help. And how about adding a wheel?"

"Yes. I thought about those things too, and I'll do them," Athena replied. "But I'm not sure how much they'll really help. I'd make the plow lighter too, but then it wouldn't cut deeply enough into the soil."

"That's a tough one," said Daedalus. He let out a deep breath. "You know, when I'm stumped for a good solution to a stubborn invention problem, it often helps me to just let go of the problem for a while. To allow a solution to bubble up in its own time."

"Interesting," said Athena. She wasn't sure how *not* thinking about a problem could actually lead to its solution, but it had been nice of him to mull over plow ideas with her. Maybe she'd take his advice. It certainly couldn't hurt! Especially since racking her brain hadn't really gotten her anywhere so far!

11
Back to MOA

LATE THAT AFTERNOON PROFESSOR LADON AND the fourteen students bid their hosts a fond farewell before boarding the blue-and-gold chariot to fly back to Mount Olympus Academy. Smoke puffed from the nostrils of the fierce-looking dragon harnessed to the chariot as Professor Ladon straddled the beast's neck and took up the reins.

"Thanks for coming, everyone!" King Minos shouted.

He stepped back as the dragon unfolded its wings and began to flap them. "Be sure to tell all your friends about the eerie—ahem, *cheery* good time you had at Minos's aMAZEment Park!"

At yet another word mix-up, Athena and Daedalus's eyes met and she was sure they were both thinking that their suspicions about the King's role in things had been right.

As the chariot lifted off, she waved to Daedalus down below. Her respect for the teenage inventor had only increased as a result of her visit. Now she saw him as a good friend as well as a world-class inventor! And they had agreed to discuss invention problems now and then, whenever a particularly puzzling one came their way.

"Good luck!" he called up to her as the chariot lifted off. Athena gave him a thumbs-up, knowing he was talking about the plow improvements she was struggling with. Her eyes searched the ground for Ariadne so she could wave to her, too, but the girl had already disappeared. Perhaps all the good-byes had been too much for her and she'd retreated to the palace. She'd been tearfully reluctant to part from Theseus during the time the chariot was being readied.

"I'll knit you a new scarf," Athena had overheard her promise him. "One you can actually wear around your neck."

"Wasn't this the best trip ever?" Pandora enthused from beside Athena as the chariot sailed off. "What was your favorite ride? Wasn't that Minotaur scary?"

Since it didn't really matter if she chose to answer all, one, or none of her roomie's questions, Athena responded to the first one. "It was an a-*maze*-ing trip." Which made Pandora giggle and launch into a new series of questions.

From the seat in front of her, Athena could hear Theseus and Heracles talking. "A little bird told me that you defeated the Minotaur after you rescued those of us stuck inside the labyrinth," she heard Heracles say. "Way to go, Cuz. You're a real *hero*!"

Despite still feeling irritated with him, Athena's lips curved a bit. That "little bird" had been her, of course.

"You know about that?" Theseus replied. Athena could hear the surprise and pleasure in his voice.

"Yes, but you can count on me to keep your secret," said Heracles.

"Because of the sword I wasn't supposed to bring?" Theseus guessed.

"Uh-huh. And also because we heroes have no real need for applause and honors, right? I mean, those things are nice, but our true satisfaction comes from helping and protecting others."

Theseus was silent for a moment. Then he said, "I see what you mean."

Athena leaned back in her seat. She and Theseus had both learned a lot on this trip, she thought. Not just about humility but about facing down their fears too. It had taken great courage for him to battle a Minotaur he'd believed to be dangerous. It had taken almost as much courage for her to admit to Daedalus that she'd made a humongous mistake with his maze. And just like she'd made a new friend in Daedalus, Theseus had become friends with—

A sharp tug on the hem of her chiton interrupted Athena's thoughts. *Huh?* She looked down to see Princess Ariadne squirm from beneath her and Pandora's seat.

"Shh," Ariadne warned both girls as she crouched at their feet.

Pandora stared down at the girl, her blue eyes wide. "What are you doing here?"

Ariadne giggled. "I'm a stowaway," she whispered.

Pandora gasped.

"Does Theseus know?" Athena whispered back. She didn't *think* he'd encourage Ariadne to smuggle herself aboard the chariot, but it never hurt to check.

"No, silly," said Ariadne. "I wanted to *surprise* him."

"He'll be surprised, all right," said Athena. "But what about your dad? Don't you think King Minos will worry when he discovers you're gone?" She was sure that Zeus would worry if she disappeared suddenly without telling him where she was going.

"I left him a note," Ariadne said defensively.

Pandora nudged the princess gently with her knee. "What did your note say?" she asked.

"That I was going to Athens to hang out with Theseus.

And that on the way I'd visit Mount Olympus Academy, too. How awesome is that!"

Pandora blinked. "Don't you know you can't come to MOA unless Principal Zeus invites you?"

Athena nodded. "True. It's my dad's rule."

"Oh," said Ariadne. She thought for a moment. "I guess I'll just go to Athens, then!" She spoke this last a little too loudly.

"Ariadne?" Theseus's head jerked around from the seat in front of the girls to look down at her in surprise. Heracles also turned to look.

"Shh," said Ariadne. But it was too late. Soon all fourteen students knew that their chariot was harboring a stowaway.

And it didn't take long for all the murmurs and exclamations of surprise to attract Professor Ladon's notice. The chariot practically went into free fall when he spotted the princess, who'd moved from the floor to squeeze onto the seat between Pandora and Athena.

After putting Artemis in temporary charge of guiding the dragon, the professor dropped down into the chariot and came to stand beside their seat. "Thisss isss not good," he told Ariadne. "If you were my daughter, I'd be ssso anxiousss for your sssafety that I wouldn't be able to sssleep until you were home again."

"Really?" Ariadne's forehead wrinkled with concern. "I don't want my dad to worry."

"Maybe if you return home now, we could convince Zeus to invite you and King Minos to MOA for a visit later on," Aphrodite suggested gently. She glanced at Athena, who nodded. If they were careful to make it seem like inviting Minos and Ariadne to the Academy was Zeus's own idea, he'd go for it for sure.

As the students looked on, Professor Ladon spoke to

Ariadne. "I'll be dropping Cassssandra off at the Immortal Marketplace, where ssshe and her family live. Then it'sss back to Crete for you," he told her sternly.

"Hey, my mom lives in the marketplace too," Theseus piped up. "She owns a travel agency called Island Dreams, and books ship passage for travelers to islands like Naxos and Crete. If you drop Ariadne and me off with Cassandra, my mom can let King Minos and my dad know where we are. Plus she can book passage home for Ariadne."

Fortunately, the professor agreed to this plan. Artemis had been guiding the chariot in a circle, waiting for a decision to be made. Now the professor relieved her of her duty, taking control of the dragon again. Under his guidance, the dragon's powerful wings caught the air, and the chariot swooped off toward the marketplace.

"I wish I didn't have to go home," Athena overheard

Theseus say to Heracles as the group approached the Immortal Marketplace. "Being with you and going on this trip was just so awesome!"

"I know," Heracles replied. "Ditto for me."

Athena felt a pang of jealousy at his reply. But she did her best to ignore it. Because, really, how would it have helped her if the two cousins *hadn't* gotten along? Despite her irritation at Heracles, she decided to be glad that he and his cousin had enjoyed each other's company. She was also glad that Theseus had gotten to play the hero, since that was so important to him.

Hoping to make him feel better about having to leave, Athena leaned across the aisle to where Cassandra and Apollo were sitting. "Can you two see some good things in Theseus's future to tell him about?" she asked.

Theseus overheard her request and whipped around. "Can you?" he asked the two fortunetellers eagerly.

Apollo and Cassandra traded smiles. "We can try," said Apollo. They were both silent for a few moments, their minds seeming to turn inward as they waited for prophecies to fill their heads.

"One day you will become a king," Apollo foretold after a while.

"Well, duh," Artemis teased him, listening in. "Since his dad is a king, it's practically a foregone conclusion that he'll be a king one day too!"

"Hey, I wasn't finished," Apollo told her. Then to Theseus he continued, "The famous playwright Euripides will someday write about you."

"Cool!" Theseus exclaimed.

"Yeah, much better, Bro," Artemis agreed, grinning at Apollo.

Athena and Cassandra exchanged glances. Theseus seemed so pleased at the idea of being written about that neither had the heart to tell him that Euripides—coincidentally the former owner of the scrollbook part of Cassandra's family's store in the marketplace—mainly wrote tragedies, not the kind of tale where all ends well.

Apollo looked at Cassandra. "Your turn."

Her nose wrinkled, and Athena thought she heard the girl murmur, "Mmm. Peppermints." The seer looked at Theseus and spoke more loudly. "You will rule dishonorably and lose great battles," she predicted.

A look of alarm came into Theseus's eyes.

"Don't worry," Athena reassured him quickly. "Remember the Opposite Oracle-O cookies? Cassandra's prophecies always turn out the opposite of what she says. So really you will rule honorably and win great battles."

"That's a relief," said Theseus, laughing.

"Yeah," agreed Ariadne.

They all hung on as the dragon suddenly took a steep, smooth dive. Looking ahead, Athena saw the high-ceilinged crystal roof of the Immortal Marketplace come into view. The IM was enormous, with rows and rows of shops separated by tall, ornate columns. Zeus's wife, Hera, had a wedding shop there, and Persephone's mom had a flower shop.

Once Professor Ladon set the chariot down on the wide slab of marble tile at the entrance to the market-place, Cassandra and Ariadne said their good-byes and took the steps down from the chariot. The two girls were already chatting excitedly about a shop called Arachne's Sewing Supplies, where Cassandra planned to take Ariadne to shop for more yarn before the princess departed for home.

Theseus slung his bag over his shoulder. Then he

gave Heracles a great big bear hug. "See you again soon, Hero-Cuz," he said.

"You too, Hero-Cuz," Heracles replied with a grin.

Theseus beamed at him. Then to Athena and the other students he called out, "Great to meet you all!" With that, he stepped from the chariot with his back straight and his head held high.

His act of heroism had added to his confidence, Athena thought. And maybe that had put his relationship with Heracles on a little more equal footing. Which wasn't a bad thing, she reflected. Having someone look up to you was nice, but it could also be a burden. It had been humbling when she'd had to admit to Daedalus that she'd made a mistake in changing his labyrinth. But admitting that had cleared the way for a real and equal friendship based on their mutual interest in invention.

Professor Ladon quickly took off again, and soon the chariot was airborne once more, flying high above the sparkling blue waters of the Aegean Sea. To pass the time Apollo made a few more predictions.

"As King Minos hoped, the park will become a huge hit," he prophesied. "When mortals hear that the Minotaur even scared a group of illustrious immortals and their mortal friends, they'll be dying to visit the park and see it for themselves."

The students burst out laughing at the irony.

"Well, it was terrifying at the time, but like I said, everyone loves a good scare," said Aphrodite.

"I wonder how all those mortals will learn about the Minotaur going crazy," Pandora asked. "No reporters came to the park, because of the conference Pheme and Eros went to, right?"

"Speaking of reporters, look!" said Actaeon.

Athena turned just in time to see a winged chariot break through the clouds. The chariot was carrying Eros, Pheme, and a few other kids who were probably also reporters. It flew parallel to them about twenty yards away. Excited to see them, Pheme waved wildly and yelled toward their dragon chariot. It was hard to hear from such a distance, though. And the wind was blowing away the cloud words she puffed overhead almost as fast as she spoke them. Still, Athena caught some of what she was saying: ". . . interview . . . you all . . . get . . . info . . . about . . . park . . ."

Pandora scurried across the aisle, taking Cassandra's former seat next to Apollo, since that side of the chariot was nearer to Pheme's chariot. She cupped her hands around her mouth and yelled, "The park was wild. What do you want to know?"

"Well, I guess that explains how news about our

a-*maze*-ing adventure is going to circulate," Apollo quipped. Which made them all laugh.

While Pandora was busy yelling a conversation back and forth with her friend Pheme, Athena took her *History of Farm Implements* scrollbook from her bag and started reading.

She looked up a few minutes later when Heracles slipped into the now empty seat beside her. He pointed at the book in her lap. "Working on a new invention?"

"Just trying to improve an old one," she replied.

"Can I help?"

"It always helps to bounce ideas around," Athena said as the chariot ascended toward Mount Olympus. Though she hadn't intended it, her words came out a bit stiffly. She still hadn't quite forgiven him for his lack of attention during the trip and for naming as his favorites the labors he'd accomplished without her. Not that she was supposed to have heard that last part. She'd been eavesdropping on his conversation with Theseus on the trip to Knossos at the time.

Heracles had left his lion cape ahead on his seat, and now he ran a hand through his dark, curly hair. "Listen," he said. "I can tell you're kind of mad at me. I'd like to fix things so we can get back to being friends again."

"Okay," she said. Her voice came out less stiffly this time. She tucked her scrollbook back into her bag and waited to see what he'd say next.

"I didn't spend as much time with you during the trip as I would have liked," he told her. "My fault for bringing Theseus, but I was just so excited to see him. It's been a long time since we've hung out."

Athena softened some. "I would have liked more time with you, too," she admitted. "But I get why you wanted to

216

hang out with Theseus. And anyway I did have fun doing the rides with my friends and talking inventor stuff with Daedalus."

"Good," said Heracles. They smiled at each other. Athena wanted to bring up his comment to Theseus regarding his favorite labors, but then, being the goddess-girl of wisdom, she wisely decided to drop the matter. It wasn't that important. Besides, weren't some of *her* favorite moments ones she'd spent alone? Like when thinking up new inventions?

"I know I'm no Daedalus," Heracles said, "but I'll give it my best shot if you want to talk about that invention you're working on."

It warmed her heart that he seemed to understand just how important being an inventor was to her, even if it was an interest they didn't really share. And thinking about that, she silently forgave him completely for valuing the labors he'd accomplished on his own over the ones she'd helped him with.

"I'm unhappy with my plow," she admitted. "If mortal farmers had your strength, it would probably work just fine. But they don't, so pushing it through fields is hard for them."

Up ahead the five-story Academy came into view. Though the sun was setting, the outlines of the majestic white stone building, which was surrounded on all sides by dozens of Ionic columns, were still visible. Against a red, purple, and pink sky, the grandeur of MOA was a sight to behold!

Heracles grinned. "Being as strong as an ox does have its advantages."

"You can say that again," said Athena.

"Being as strong as an ox does—"

"That's it!" she interrupted him suddenly, her eyes

lighting up. As Professor Ladon guided the dragon chariot toward the courtyard below, she added, "That's the
answer!"

Heracles cocked his head at her. "You just figured
out how to improve that plow of yours, didn't you?" He
reached over and took her hand in his.

Athena nodded happily, both because she'd solved
her invention problem *and* because Heracles was holding her hand.

"That's one of the things I like about you," he told her
fondly. "Those wheels inside your brain are always turning. But if you aren't too busy inventing stuff tomorrow,
maybe we can go get shakes at the Supernatural Market?"

She squeezed his fingers, grinning. "Sure!"

As the dragon chariot set down in the courtyard,
Artemis's dogs came running to meet it. Seeing them
reminded Athena of how funny Nectar had looked when

he'd gotten her papyrus "wheel" stuck around his neck earlier that week. And that's when she got *another* great idea. "Ye gods," she murmured.

"Um . . . Earth to Athena," Heracles said, interrupting her thoughts. She'd been so lost in them that she hadn't noticed when he'd stood up to put on his cape and grab both their bags. Everyone else had already left the chariot. Now he stood waiting for her to exit it ahead of him.

"Oh, sorry!" Athena beamed at him as she jumped up. "But I just got the best idea! I'll design a yoke to link two oxen together. Pulling a plow is hard for one man but would be light work for even one ox, given how strong they are. For *two* oxen the work would be lighter still."

"Awesome!" he said, sounding really happy for her.

"Yeah, I don't know why that didn't occur to me before.

After all, it's common for animals to help pull chariots. I just thought of it now when I saw Artemis's dogs."

She couldn't wait to flesh out her yoke design, which would keep the oxen heading in the same direction while fitting comfortably around their necks. However, all that could wait till later. Heracles easily hefted both of their bags onto one shoulder, then helped her leap down from the chariot. Not that she needed his help, but it was still nice of him.

Once they were down, she slipped her hand into his. Swinging their hands between them, she and Heracles headed across the courtyard, back to good old MOA. Up ahead Pheme and Pandora were walking side by side, their heads together as they climbed the granite steps that led into the school.

Athena smiled inwardly. When Pheme's next column in *Teen Scrollazine* came out, it wouldn't be long till every mortal and immortal knew of the fourteen students' adventures in Crete!

Laughter floated back to Heracles and her from the other students walking in front of them. Aphrodite was teasing Ares. Apollo and Artemis were having one of their typical brother-sister disagreements, laced with giggles. And Medusa and Dionysus were talking in quiet tones. It was a magical night. Tomorrow would be magical too. She and Heracles were finally, at looong last, going to get to hang out! Yes!

Two weeks later . . .

DEAR DAEDALUS,

I JUST WANTED TO LET YOU KNOW

THAT YOUR ADVICE TO LET GO OF

STUBBORN INVENTION PROBLEMS AND

ALLOW SOLUTIONS TO BUBBLE UP IN

THEIR OWN TIME REALLY WORKED!

FARMERS WRITE THAT MY NEW

INVENTION OF THE YOKE, WHICH KEEPS

TWO OXEN PULLING IN THE SAME

DIRECTION, WORKS GREAT. IT'S LIGHT

WORK FOR THESE STRONG ANIMALS TO

PULL THE PLOW. NOW FARMERS NEED

ONLY WALK BEHIND AND GUIDE IT. THEY

SAY THAT CULTIVATING THEIR FIELDS

HAS NEVER BEEN EASIER AND THAT THEY

CAN PLANT MORE CROPS THAN EVER BEFORE AND FEED MANY MORE PEOPLE AND ANIMALS.

I SO ENJOYED BEING IN CRETE. THE AMAZEMENT PARK IS TERRIFICALLY FUN, AND YOUR LABYRINTH IS PERFECT NOW AND NEEDS NO IMPROVEMENTS. ☺

IT WAS A TREAT TO SPEND TIME WITH A FELLOW INVENTOR. YOU TAUGHT ME A LOT, AND NOT JUST ABOUT INVENTIONS.

YOUR FRIEND,

ATHENA

Don't miss the next adventure in
the *Goddess Girls* series!

Coming Soon